A Love So Bright

Insomniac Duet - Book Two

PERSEPHONE AUTUMN

BETWEEN WORDS PUBLISHING LLC

*To those who have been knocked down, then got back on their feet
and said "not today, bitch."
This one is for you.*

<u>Bay Area Duet Series</u>

<u>Click Duet</u>

Through the Lens

Time Exposure

<u>Inked Duet</u>

Fine Line

Love Buzz

<u>Insomniac Duet</u>

Restless Night

A Love So Bright

<u>Artist Duet</u>

Blank Canvas (Fall 2022)

Abstract Passion (Fall 2022)

<u>Devotion Series</u>

Distorted Devotion

Undying Devotion

Beloved Devotion

Darkest Devotion

<u>Standalone Romance Novels</u>

Depths Awakened

Sweet Tooth

Transcendental

<u>Poetry Collections</u>

Ink Veins

Broken Metronome

<u>Standalone Horror Novels</u>

By Dawn (published under P. Autumn)

ONE

MICAH

"I'M PREGNANT, asshole. And you're going to be a daddy," the blonde—whose name I don't remember—shouts.

My feet stumble backward until I bump the back counter. The earth quakes beneath my feet. And no matter how deep I inhale, air refuses to fill my lungs. I shake my head, refusing to believe a word this woman says.

A loud clang rings out and I snap my head to the left. Peyton stands frozen in place, the broom handle on the ground. Her eyes wide and mouth agape.

Shit. Fuck.

Peyton doesn't move, doesn't breathe. Her eyes locked on the woman spewing lies on the opposite side of the bar. All the color has drained from Peyton's face. Her hands tremble at her sides. Any moment, she may explode with fury. Question is, will that fury be directed at me?

I need to fix this. Now.

"Sorry to break the news to you, but I always wrap up.

Go trap some other random guy you hooked up with." I fold my arms over my chest, widen my stance, and hold my ground. Appearing more confident than I feel.

The woman throws her head back and laughs. Laughs. Like she has secret intel. "Condoms aren't always a hundred-percent effective."

She didn't own or discount sleeping around. Note to self. "You don't look pregnant." I wave a hand toward her skintight, come-fuck-me dress. "You on the prowl for another man to trap?" She grinds her jaw as her face reddens. "Until you have legal proof of what you're claiming, you need to leave."

The woman slams her palms on the bar and shrieks. A few people linger as Roar prepares to close, but their eyes don't deviate from the madness. I don't move or react to her obvious attempt at baiting me. And it seems to bother her more.

Oh. Fucking. Well.

Yes, it's true, I have slept with a shit ton of women. Maybe two or three different women per week over the last year plus. The title manwhore was earned—not that I am proud. But I swear to whatever deity listens, I never went without a condom. Ever. And each one that got tossed in the trash was intact. If it wasn't, the woman would have known then and there, and other preventive measures would have commenced.

Which is why I refuse to believe this woman. No doubt she slept with some schmuck she can't pin down. Next easiest resolution, nail it on a guy you can find.

Sorry, bitch. Not happening.

After minutes of not caving, she grunts, pushes away from the bar and heads for the door. But not before calling over her shoulder. "You'll see me again. Count on it." Then she disappears.

Thank fuck.

For the first time in what seems like hours, I breathe. I turn to face Peyton and notice she hasn't moved. At all. Is she breathing?

Shit.

"Hey," I say and lift my hands to frame her face. She doesn't respond. Her eyes vacant and off in the distance. "Peyton?" I step in front of her, crowd her, so she will look me in the eye, and stroke my thumbs over her cheeks. "Peyton, look at me."

I stop breathing. My eyes refuse to deviate from hers. Then, she blinks several times as if waking from a deep sleep. Her usual fiery violet irises are duller as they refocus. My thumbs continue to stroke her cheeks as she starts to shake her head. When her chin wobbles, my pulse jolts.

"I need to go," she mutters.

"What?"

"Micah…" Her eyes glaze over as she tucks her lips between her teeth. "I… I need to go."

Go? What does she mean she needs to go? Go where?

Maybe she needs to sit down and breathe a minute. Shake off the crazy bitch that flew in and stormed out. If I were her, I would need time to process what just went down.

"Why don't you go sit in the office. I'll finish up out here. Then we can head out."

Glassy violet irises whip to my starry blues. "No, Micah." Her breathing picks up. Lungs heaving as if they can't pull in enough oxygen. "I need to go *home*. Knew this was a bad idea."

She starts to step away from me, but I catch her elbow. "Peyton." Her name is a plea for mercy on my tongue. "Please, just come back to my place. We can talk about this." I point toward the door. "There is no possible way that woman is pregnant by me. Or any woman, for that matter."

Realization of how loud this conversation is has my eyes sweeping the club. I breathe easier when I see everyone has left. Well, the patrons are gone. The remaining staff has scattered to give us privacy.

"How can you be so sure? I'm no rocket scientist, Micah, but even I know the tiniest pinprick can lead to pregnancy."

Jesus fucking Christ.

Why is she on this other woman's side? Is it the whole "women band together" thing? Because in this situation, that is complete and utter bullshit. Not when one of the women is shady as fuck.

If Peyton walks away from me now, I have a feeling I won't stand a chance in the future. Again. No matter what, we can't go separate ways tonight. Not with this fake ass shit lingering in the air. Not without talking this through and seeing reason.

"Peyton." Her name is a whisper on my tongue as I step back into her space. "This whole situation is a cluster-fuck. But I know, without a shadow of doubt, there is no possible way that woman is pregnant with *my* child. Not a chance. So, please…" I fully invade her space. Bring my lips to her ear. Feel her tremble beneath me as I rest my hands on her arms. "Please, don't do this. Don't walk away. Don't shut me out. Not without giving me a chance. Not without giving *us* a chance."

For day-long seconds, she remains a statue in my arms. Stoic and silent. Her hot breath on my neck the only reminder this is real. That this isn't an epic nightmare —at least not the type to vanish when you open your eyes. This nightmare is manageable. It would be more manageable if Peyton took my side. If she believed the truth. *My truth.*

Do pregnancies happen when condoms are worn? All the time.

But I am no damn fool. Maybe off my rocker at times, but not a fool. The guy in the contraceptive aisle inspecting the condom boxes with hardcore scrutiny… yep, that would be Micah Reed. The guy who opens the box when he gets home and examines every wrapper for any cuts, tears or holes. That would also be me. Condoms don't go in my wallet unless I am one-hundred-percent sure they are tamper-free. Hell, I even buy the ones with spermicide.

Don't care what the woman said, her baby—if she is actually pregnant—doesn't share my DNA.

Peyton fights an internal battle. Her fingers ball into fists, then relax, over and over. Much as I don't want her to walk away from me tonight, she gets to make the decision to stay or go. What is happening between us is fresh, new. Wouldn't surprise me if she took a step back and told me to fuck off. That she didn't sign up for this.

But I really want her to step up and fight. Stick with me as we navigate our feelings. Then, give in to those emotions. Allow me to give in to mine.

For far too long, Peyton has consumed my thoughts. I suspected the moment I had a chance with her, I would shred her clothes and relish my name on her tongue.

The moment my lips crashed down on hers, though... it was as if my synapses fired right for the first time. Pieces fell into place and life started to make sense. And if I felt all that after one kiss, I fantasize what life may be like after I taste more than her lips. More serious and intense. Addictive and engrossing. I won't be able to stay away from her.

Which is why *I'm* not ready to have sex with Peyton.

Hands brush the sides of my torso and snake around my waist to connect at my lower back. I inhale deeply for the first time in minutes. Let the cool air fill my lungs and settle my anxiety. Allow my body to relax and melt with hers.

"I'll come back to your place under one condition," she

whispers in my ear. "We talk. That's it. Tonight will not be a rerun of last night."

I nod. This, I accept… with one slight variation. "Can we at least grab food?" I lean back, sweep wayward strands of hair from her face, and brush my knuckles down her cheek. "Microwave meals from the store or order delivery. Don't care which. But we should eat."

"That's fine." She looks to the broom on the ground. "We should finish up and close."

I don't want to free her from my hold, but we will never leave otherwise. So I loosen my grip and step back. I drop a kiss on her forehead, take a deep breath and nod.

We get back to work and finish our nightly tasks. Twenty minutes fly by faster than expected and it isn't long before we say good night to the staff walking out the door with us. I tell Peyton I will order Chinese and pick it up on the way to the house. After she gives me her order, she hops in her car and drives out of the lot.

As her taillights disappear, an odd sensation slithers up my spine, spreads through my limbs and I shiver head to toe. The sensation eats me alive like a microbial plague. Makes me second-guess Peyton's reason to come over tonight. Acid rises in my throat and I swallow to stanch it from exiting my lips.

It's all in your head, man. Don't make something out of nothing.

After several deep breaths, I call the Chinese joint near my house. I order more than either of us will eat, but plan to have leftovers for another meal or two. Once the order is placed, I take one last deep breath, death grip the steering wheel, and drive off.

When I hit the bridge, I pray the salty air whipping my face and filling my lungs will untwist this knife in my gut. Will loosen the knot gradually getting tighter with each mile my truck eats up. Will vanquish the overall bad feeling swallowing me whole.

No matter how many breaths I take, no matter how I steer my thoughts, the pang beneath my diaphragm doesn't fade. If anything, the knife twists deeper. Grinds my bones and digs into the marrow.

Please, let this be my imagination running wild. Don't let the beginning of what we have go to shit. Not over this.

I repeat this again and again. A dictum to reign over what will come of tonight. A precept to dictate the future, regardless of the irrationality steering my thoughts. Because if you repeat something enough times, if you put the energy out into the universe, it becomes truth. Not like prophecy. More like guidance down the path of my choosing.

The red-dress woman made an attempt to derail my life, my future, tonight. Tried to trap me with a pregnancy scare. But she won't rattle me so easily. She won't cuff me at the ankle and drag me beside her. Not without hard proof. And until that day arrives, I will live my life. On my terms.

Who knows what my future holds. If Peyton is a part of said future, I will be forever indebted to her and whatever celestial being grants me the opportunity. An opportunity to right the wrongs I have committed. An opportunity to see where our connection leads.

"Thank you," I mutter into the wind. "Whoever is looking out for me, thank you."

I won't let you down.

TWO

PEYTON

WHY THE HELL am I here? Why did I agree to this?

Agreeing to meet Micah at his house after what just happened is not a good idea. Especially with my mind all over the place. I don't know which way is up or whose truth to believe. Anger and frustration and anguish claw me up one side and down the other. My guardian angel has one hand on her hip while she wags a finger from the other in my face. The words *I told you so* on the tip of her tongue.

I want to heed her advice and drive off before Micah gets home. Save my heart from another walk down Shitty Life Lane. Yet, here I am. Waiting. A glutton for punishment.

I press the heel of my palm to my breastbone and rub. Do my best to sooth the ache and simmer the heightened sting. One by one, my heart leaks every ounce of hope and joy and possibility I had for Micah. Spills it at my feet.

And I simply watch it puddle before it seeps into the earth.

Fuck.

When it comes to me, Micah Reed breeds misfortune.

As a young woman, I pined for him. Watched him from afar on the track. Peeked his direction whenever he was near. Even after he crushed my soul with his words, even after he made a mockery of me in front of half the school, I still yearned for his affection. For his attention. For any fondness he would bestow upon me.

Then, I grew up.

The memory of him always sat in the shadows of my mind, but I moved on. Found people who knew my worth. Knew I wasn't just some loner girl with a crazy obsession for all things black. Knew I had more to give. And those people surrounded me with smiles and laughter and love. They lifted me up and brought me back to life. Showed me real friendship and what it meant to care for others. I owe them more than I will ever be able to give.

So why the hell am I here?

Why did I willingly choose to walk into the lion's den? Why am I setting myself up for more pain? More pain inflicted by Micah Reed.

"Because I'm a fucking idiot," I whisper into the dark cab of my SUV.

Unlike last night, Micah's house holds no interest. I don't stare at the shrubs and flowering plants along the front and try to guess what they are. I don't stare at the wood fence and wonder what setup he has beyond the wall of windows. I don't have the energy to care. Not tonight. Not after the wake-up call from Little Miss Red Dress.

Not focusing on anything in particular, I stare toward the end of the street. Let my eyes glaze over as they land on the yellow diamond sign that reads *no outlet*. Space out and let my mind blank as I wait.

Before long, Micah's headlights beam around the corner and blind me in the rearview mirror. Once he parks in the driveway, I move my car to park behind him. He hops out of his truck with two hefty bags of food and waits for me to join him.

Here we go.

The thirteen steps from his driveway to the front door feel like miles. Neither of us says a word as he unlocks the door, flips the light on and gestures me toward the couch. He sets the bags on the table, kisses the top of my head and wanders down the hall to what I presume is his bedroom.

Twenty-one breaths later, he settles on the couch, his leg brushing mine. Silence dominates the room like a deprivation chamber. And with each passing tick of the clock, a new pin gets pushed into the voodoo doll made to inflict me with pain.

Cursed. That's what this is. My life curse. If not, I am all ears for some other logical explanation. Some magical reason as to why I can't seem to hold on to… love, happiness, anything worthwhile.

I don't *love* Micah. It is way too soon to feel such a

powerful emotion. But I do like him. More than I imagined possible after all the hurt he caused.

But every person I get romantically close to… the relationship always goes south. Every. Single. Time.

Am I destined to be a loner hag? A cat lady minus the cats. Always just me, myself and I as my hair turns gray and wrinkles define my face more than my expression.

As a little girl, I don't remember a time when I played dress-up, pretended to marry the boy up the street, and have babies in our perfect house with the perfect yard. I never fantasized about a prince sweeping me off my feet and rescuing me from tragedy. I didn't dream of a happily ever after and forever love. It just wasn't who I was.

But as years passed, my perspective on life shifted. I see things in a different light and with occasional filters. I wonder what would happen if I took a leap, tried something new, explored all the possibilities.

I don't want to spend my life alone. But I also don't want the heartache that comes with giving your all to another person.

And with Micah's history, heartache has an open-ended invitation.

Carton by carton, he pulls the food from bags. Sets a small container of shrimp egg foo young, rice and gravy in front of me on the coffee table. Places a fork and chopsticks on top.

"Hungry?" I choke out as Micah removes another four cartons and a container of soup.

He gives a timid smile. "I like leftovers. Makes my life easier."

Life probably won't be so easy for the next however many months. I want to say this to him. Want to tell him just because he says the baby—real or not—isn't his, doesn't make it true. Only science will prove one way or the other. And as crazy as the woman was in Roar, I don't picture her backing down. She will return, with a smug smile on her face. She will be a constant smack in the face, a constant reminder of who Micah was before.

I open the cartons and poke at the food. Eat a few small bites. Taste the egg, shrimp and vegetable pancakes, but don't savor them. Not like I usually do. When I peek at Micah from the corner of my eye, he appears to be in the same predicament. Half an egg roll eaten, some missing lo mein noodles, and a few slurps of egg drop soup gone.

"Micah..." He sets the egg roll down on the wrapper, wipes his hands clean, then meets my gaze. His eyes are veiny and damp. The starry flecks less visible in his dark-sky irises. "We have to talk about this."

Have to, versus want to, are two different animals.

I don't *want* to talk about the possibility of some random woman being pregnant from the guy I just started spending time with. We just sorted out our differences. He apologized and I mentally forgave him sometime over the last two weeks. Things between us were headed in a good direction. And now we *need* to talk about this.

We need to talk about the *what-ifs*.

"Yeah, we do." He huffs and sags into the couch. "For the record, though, this sucks."

This does suck. Hairy, sweaty, nasty balls.

He sits back up, plants his elbows on his knees, then leans forward and hangs his head. His broad shoulders stretch the cotton of his shirt. Put the definition of his muscles and stress on display. I swallow at the sight. My fingers itch to reach out. To trace the lines of tension in his neck and upper back and soothe his suffering. I lift a hand, then hesitate. Resist temptation. Drop my hand, curl my fingers into fists at my sides and force them to stay put.

Micah may need comfort right now, but so do I. This situation may not be directly impacting me, but it impacts me nonetheless.

"What if she is pregnant?" I pose the first of many questions.

He sits straighter. "She might be." He twists to face me and our knees knock. "But I won't believe anything without proof."

This I understand. If I were in his shoes, I would want hard evidence too. To be present as the tests are performed. Receive my own letter of proof when the results become available. Micah may have slept with his fair share of the female population, but I believe him when he says he practiced safety measures.

"What if tests prove the baby is yours?" I wince as the words leave my lips.

My reaction may give the vibe I don't care for children. Couldn't be further from the truth. I love their chubby cheeks and chunky legs. Love their expressions and laughter when you make faces or speak in different tones. Love how soft they are and how good they smell. Their innocence and untainted view of the world. Babies and young children are just happy.

But the idea of potentially dating someone while another woman carries his child... not sure I have the strength to handle it.

Micah reaches for my hand and I let him take it. He cocoons it in both of his. I focus on the warmth of his touch. The way his thumbs draw small circles over the top of my hand. And how he stares at our joined hands as if scared they will disappear if he looks away.

"Don't think it will." He lifts his red eyes. "But if the baby is mine, I'll take responsibility." I jerk my hand back, but Micah doesn't release me from his grip. "That doesn't mean anything changes between us, Peyton."

I love and hate that he won't let me go. That he refuses to surrender to outside forces. That he plans to fight for what he wants, but will still do the right thing in the end if need be.

The Micah in front of me isn't the same from my teenage years. Teenage Micah was more selfish and did whatever benefited his life the most. Adult Micah still has some of these same tendencies, but knows when to step up and be a man. When to do the right thing, but not let anyone rob him of life and the prospect of love.

"I want to believe you. God, Micah, I really do. But

you can't deny a baby would flip your world upside down."

"Not denying it. But life is what we make it. If this woman *is* pregnant with *my* child, I will do my part. Doing my part does *not* equal being in a relationship with her." Fingers brush the underside of my chin and lift. Our eyes lock. Neither of us breathes. "If I haven't made it obvious yet, I want a relationship with *you*."

You know what they say about assuming… and I am definitely not going to assume with Micah Reed. Not when it comes to matters of the heart. Not when he has the ability to squash me like a bug and walk away unscathed.

His fingers drop away from my chin. Then his knuckles brush along my cheek. I sigh, and my entire frame caves forward. There will always be a piece of me that is weak for Micah. A part always ready to crumple to his demands, his will. This doesn't necessarily make me weak as a woman. Just weak when it comes to making informative, clear-minded decisions regarding him.

And I cannot afford to be weak.

"Let's eat," I suggest. My appetite may not have returned, but I hate food waste.

Micah flips on the television, but neither of us pays attention as our food slowly disappears. Dinner tonight is riddled with silence and anxiety and stress over what the future holds. Not only *my* future with Micah but also his if he becomes a father. Like it or not, fatherhood will change his life more than he realizes.

When I can't eat another bite, I close up the containers and put them in one of the bags. "I should go."

I need time alone to process this evening's news. And maybe some best-friend time to mull it over. When too close to a situation, it's always better to talk with someone not in the thick of it. Someone you trust and will listen to when they give advice.

"Sorry," Micah mumbles as we rise from the couch.

"For what?"

"Fucking this up. Seems to be my specialty." He laughs without humor as I lead us to the door. "But I'll make it better. I swear."

I don't doubt his proclamation. Micah is the type to go after what he wants. If what he wants happens to be yours truly, it will happen. Doesn't mean I won't make him work for it, though.

Before I get out the door, before I stop him from stepping closer, Micah crushes my lips with a smoldering kiss. And for one, two, three vicious beats of my pulse, I remain stone cold. Frigid as he tries to coax a kiss in return. The softness of his lips, the warmth of his arms circling my waist, and the sweet woodsy scent of his cologne... the triple whammy makes me surrender. I fist his shirt and haul him closer. Kiss him as if this may be the last time — because who knows what tomorrow will bring.

My body says to never let go. But my mind tells me to stop, take a step back, and leave. To get out of here before my feet refuse to go. Difficult as it is, I break the kiss. I unclench my fingers and turn my back to Micah.

"I should go," I mutter and twist the knob.

From the door to the car, the only noise to fill the silence is the clack of my heels and the soft thumps of Micah's bare feet hitting the ground. No buzzing insects. No wind gusts to rustle the leaves. No chatty neighbors or rumbling car engines. Nothing but undiluted silence. An awkward, unbearable silence until I unlock the car.

I start the car and roll down the window. "Thanks for dinner."

He reaches forward, his knuckles brush down my cheek. "Sorry it wasn't as great as last night."

God, this is so weird. Why does this have to be so fucking weird? "I better go."

With a solemn nod, he takes one, two steps back. "Drive safe. See you tomorrow."

I roll up my window, back out of the driveway, and watch as Micah disappears in my rearview mirror. The moment he vanishes, a fist tightens around my heart as the floodgates open and spill down my cheeks. I drive the short distance home in a mental and visual blur. The minute I walk through the front door and Reese takes one look at me, two warm arms engulf me.

This annihilates the dam wall on my emotions. My frame shakes as I drench Reese's shirt. He hugs me impossibly tighter, rubs a gentle hand up and down my spine, and shushes me as we rock in place. My purse hits the floor with a thump, and my keys clang when they land next. At some point, without me realizing, Reese walks us to the couch and sets me in his lap.

After hour-long minutes, the tears form dry salt lines to my chin. Snot clogs my nose and stains Reese's shirt. My throat withered; eyes puffy and achy. My heart an ashy mold waiting for the breeze to blow it to dust.

Reese holds me close while his one hand continues its journey up and down my spine. Every other stroke up, he stops to tuck a strand of hair behind my ear or run his fingers through the strands.

"Talk to me, sunshine," he whispers, his breath warm and comforting at my temple.

I inch back and stare into kind brown eyes. Eyes full of love and sincerity. More times than I can count, Reese has held my hand. Been my stronghold or lifted me up. Been there for me without judgment or conditions. No matter what bullshit life throws at either of us, our friendship never crumbles. As if fate knew I needed someone to love me in every way except romantically.

Reese is my person, and I am his. Day or night, through thick and thin, we are there for each other.

I spill every unsettling second about tonight. About the woman and how Micah reacted to the whole situation. How the entire scenario felt like a dull knife pushing into my rib cage. How the knife twisted each time Micah denied the possibility. And how the knife gutted me when Micah wanted to go about things as if the woman never stepped foot in Roar.

"My sweet Peyton." Reese hugs me close again. "I understand your pain and frustration with all this." He releases me and leans back to look into my eyes. "But if I were in his shoes, I'd be equally defensive. Especially if I took every precaution."

"Are you seriously taking his side?" I whine and narrow my eyes.

Warmth wraps my hand as Reese takes it in his. "This isn't about sides, sunshine. First of all, you'll always be number one. Always. Second, stop and really think about it. Put yourself in his position. If someone approached you and told you something equally life changing, wouldn't you question it?" I teeter my head left and right. "The answer is yes. We've known each other too many years to say otherwise."

He has me there. For obvious reasons, I can't put myself in Micah's shoes. Me impregnating someone is impossible. But if someone accused me of something heinous that I felt was inconceivable, I would deny it without evidence too.

"This is one of a long list of reasons why I need you. You know me. You explain it from different views until I have more than one perspective." I huff out a deep breath and my shoulders cave inward. "Not that it resolves how I feel, but thank you."

Reese pats my hand. "Don't drive yourself crazy thinking about it. But don't let it go without giving it genuine thought. It's a big deal, but not the end of the world. No sense in worrying over something that may not hold merit."

I rise from his lap and he stands too. "Thanks for always being here. Don't know what I'd do without you." I wrap my arms around his neck and hug him hard.

His arms circle my waist and hug with equal strength. "Live a boring life, I'm sure." I drop a hand and poke his ribs. "Argh! It was a joke. Geez."

"Ha ha," I deadpan. I pick up my purse and keys from the floor and start for the hall. "Going to try and get some sleep. Night."

"Sleep tight, sunshine. I'll make us French toast in the morning."

I press a hand to my heart. "With extra powdered sugar?"

"Always."

After changing into a knee-length nightshirt, I slip under the covers and close my eyes. Sleep doesn't take me quickly, like usual. Instead, my brain clicks on and evaluates every possible outcome to several scenarios. An hour of mental torment passes, and I have no viable answers. I can't.

Because I don't know Micah well enough to know what he would do. Nor what the truth is when it comes to the red-dress woman.

So, I do my best to let it go. Let go of an outcome I have no control of. Let go of a future I can't predict. Let go of the what-ifs and fabricated scenarios my mind created.

"You look like shit."

Nothing like bluntness when you need softer edges. "Thanks, Aunt Leanne. I love you, too," I say with a dash of sarcasm as I slide into the booth across from her.

Monday has always been our day. Lunch after I leave Gulfside. An hour or two of girl time as we catch up on life. My weekly dose of Dad's side of the family. But with the new change in my work schedule and last night's bullshit, I need to see her today.

"Don't get your panties in a bunch. All I meant is you seem exhausted."

Exhaustion is a good word to explain how I feel. My limbs are heavier than Corinthian pillars. Eyes swollen, veiny and dry. My mind spends so much time in the fog, I'd swear we lived near the San Francisco Bay rather than Tampa Bay. And my heart… well, my heart currently teeters on barbed wire. Sleep was a joke last night; or should I say this morning. I may have slept three hours max as I tried my damnedest to let go. Easier said than done.

"Yeah, yesterday was rough. Glad you could meet up."

Aunt Leanne reaches across the table and covers my hand with hers. "Me, too. Now let's get some food and talk."

We study the menu and pick out lunch as the server

approaches the table. Once we place our orders, I sip my water while Aunt Leanne lifts a brow and waits for me to spill every detail.

In so many ways, Aunt Leanne reminds me of Dad. Her bluntness and no-nonsense attitude. But also, her never-ending patience and practical mind. Whenever life feels off-kilter, Aunt Leanne uses her saintlike restraint and listens to every word. Just like Dad did. She lets me spill all the crazy details, then sits quietly for a bit and lets my words marinate. Figures out which parts are most important and starts there first.

"Remember the guy at work I told you about?"

She studies my eyes a beat. "Mmhm."

"Well, a couple nights ago, we kissed. And not your basic peck. More the hot and heavy kind."

Just like Dad and Aunt Leanne, I don't beat around the bush either. Some conversations are tougher to have, but they spill out sooner or later.

"Why do I get the feeling this kiss was great then, but isn't now?"

I take a deep breath and hold it to the count of five. "Because last night at work, some woman came in and claimed to be pregnant with his baby."

Aunt Leanne chokes on her sip of water. *Jesus, Peyton. Could you not have waited until she swallowed first?* I jump up from my seat and smack her back over her lungs. She waves me away as the coughing slows.

"Damn, girl. Trying to kill me?"

I purse my lips and raise my brows. "Hope you're being sarcastic, 'cause that's not remotely funny."

"Sorry." She coughs one last time, then takes another sip of water. "Of all the scenarios I expected, that was definitely not one of them. Took me by surprise, is all."

"Just be glad you didn't witness it firsthand."

The corners of her mouth turn down as her lower lip juts out slightly. Some may confuse the look with pity, but I recognize the fraction of heartbreak she has for me in this moment. With all the painful tragedies of my past, adding another to the list sucks.

"It probably hurts, but tell me everything. From start to finish."

So, until our lunch arrives, I regale her with the events of the last forty-eight hours. Tell her the good news with work, Micah's reaction, and mine in turn. The kiss in the office and later at his house. I share how happy and weightless it felt to be around him, and the potential of what the future holds.

Then, I go into the bomb drop. How worked up this woman was about Micah not accepting her word. I share how the woman looked ready to party, and take another random man to her bed. And then, how I went back to Micah's house to talk. Our awkward silence and kiss before I said good night. How I felt empty and broken the moment I drove away.

Our plates slide in front of us and I snag a fry from my plate to munch on. As per usual, Aunt Leanne goes quiet after my story. She eats her BLT and I eat my fish sandwich. I pick at my fries and she eats her pineapple coleslaw. When our plates are empty, Aunt Leanne pushes hers aside and clasps her hands on the table.

"I assume you asked me here today because you want advice."

Mimicking her movement, I push my plate aside and lean forward. "That and to see if you think I'm overreacting. Is it weird for me to presume she's telling the truth? To think Micah should act differently?"

Taking my hands in hers, she rubs back and forth. "No reaction is wrong, Peyton. We all see and hear and feel and react to things in our own way. Just because it's different than someone else's reaction doesn't make it right or wrong. Your reaction is your own."

"I hate that instinct has me leaning away from him instead of standing closer."

She releases my hands, but doesn't stray far. "Sweetheart, you two have history. One that has messed with you for years. I'd find it odd if you *didn't* feel the way you do." My brows shoot to my hairline. "Just because you played tonsil hockey with the man, it doesn't erase history."

"Tonsil hockey? Seriously?" Feels like I'm a kid again.

Laughter floats in the air as tears spill down Aunt Leanne's face. "Would you rather I say sucking face? Or swapping spit? Canoodling, perhaps?" I drop my head in my hands. "Doesn't matter what you call it, you've had your tongue down the man's throat."

Jesus. Heat surges up my chest to my neck and face. No doubt my cheeks look more like pomegranate skin. I lift my gaze enough to see no one is paying us any attention. Thank god. Then sip my water in the hopes it will cool down the heat of embarrassment.

"Where were we?" I ask once I drain the water glass.

"Having good weeks with a person doesn't erase the bad years in your memory. You may enjoy his company now, but you still have barriers in place. Protection measures, in case he messes up again. By the sounds of it, you've already got the razor wire in place and the gate closing around your heart."

The waiter stops at the table to check on us and clear our plates. A thirty-second break in our conversation. Enough time to ponder what to say next. The moment he walks off, Aunt Leanne perches her chin on her hands and waits with eager eyes.

"If you were me, what would you do?"

"Obviously, I never experienced *your* pain years ago. But if I were in your shoes, I'd give myself a little time. Nowadays, everyone feels decisions have to be made immediately. That no one should have to wait. In some situations, this may be true. But in others, time is what you need. Especially when it's personal."

"So, I should give it time?" Time to sink in? Or time apart? This is so damn confusing.

This is why relationships are a pain in the ass. Don't get me wrong, I love sharing a connection with someone. Love not wanting to be apart from them. But drama and uncertainty are not qualities I want to embrace in a relationship.

"Give yourself time to really grasp the situation. Look at it from your perspective. Then, look at it from his. Write down your feelings on each. Imagine how you'd feel if someone threw news like this in your face and expected you to halt your life and cater to them. Let yourself *feel* what it'd be like to be in that scenario. Then make a decision from there."

Wise beyond her years, just like her brother had been. This is the reason—among several others—why I ask Aunt Leanne all the hard questions. Why I bring up the life-changing stuff with her. Not that Mom wouldn't give sage advice. Mom's advice just happens to slant toward whatever is easiest. And easy isn't always the best choice.

"Thank you. You always know how to make me see situations with fresh eyes."

"Glad to help." She pats my hand and scoots out of the booth. "Now let's get out of here. You need to nap before work."

I chuckle at her vague way of telling me I look like shit again. But I wouldn't want this woman any other way. There are few people in this world whose opinions matter to me. Aunt Leanne gives it to me like it is, straight and to the point, and I appreciate it each and every time.

We hug near my car. "See you Monday?" she asks.

"Yeah. My schedule changed, but lunch is still good. Maybe an hour earlier?"

She kisses my cheek. "Sounds good. Keep me posted until then. Love you."

"Love you, too."

I hop in my car and press the ignition. For a moment, I stare out the windshield and lose focus. *"Look at it from your perspective. Then, look at it from his."* Call it my homework assignment, but I need to sit down and really evaluate us and both sides of the coin.

No matter what happens in the end, no matter what I choose, I trust my intuition won't lead me down the wrong path. Not again.

THREE

MICAH

THE LONGER PEYTON IS SILENT, the more I wither at the seams.

Yesterday, she walked in the back door of Roar, set her belongings in a locker, threw me a half-assed smile, and got to work. I had sent her a text in the morning—like I had for weeks—and got no response. All night, she slung drinks behind the bar and laughed with patrons. But the moment she glanced my way, an impossible wall erected between us.

I hate walls. But she needs space. I get it.

Does space equal zero interaction? No standard greeting or cordial exchanges. Fuck if I know. But her avoidance is the slowest, most torturous death. Like getting thrown on the rack, limbs bound at the wrists and ankles, torso stabilized, and, inch by inch, my starfished body gets stretched to its limit.

"Hey, boss," Ted says as I approach the front. "You good?"

Irritates me to no end that people read my emotions without a word. It isn't my nature to flaunt my feelings. Yet, I don't shut down or dodge them. But having my heart on my sleeve—at work, no less—is an open invitation for questions. Questions I have no desire to answer.

"Yeah, man. Just got a lot on my mind is all." The two seconds I pause to take a breath, Ted opens his mouth to speak. But I beat him to it. "Things good here?" I point toward the door.

He nods, then prattles on about the few people who tried to get in without paying cover or were underage. His voice hangs in the atmosphere, but I don't absorb a word. Not when I spot Peyton across the club, smiling and laughing with two guys.

How many days had passed since she smiled at me with gaiety? Two. Two decades-long days. And I hated every single, solitary second of those two days.

Ted stops talking and I have enough sense to notice. I pat his shoulder, force a smile, and leave him to stroll the perimeter of Roar with Peyton in my periphery. Her champagne locks secured in a high ponytail, I recall the silky gloss of the strands. Her laughter floats across the club as flashes of her under me as I tickled her ribs invade my vision.

Fuck.

When was the last time I focused so much attention on

one woman? Let her occupy my every waking and sleeping thought.

Sadly, the answer to that question comes too quick. Rochelle.

Rochelle Cook was the only woman I let consume me. In every way possible. She lured me in and sank her perfectly manicured claws into my heart until every drop of blood dried at her feet. I hadn't realized it at the time, but my entire life revolved around her and her needs.

Until the day she drove her five-inch heel through my heart and left me a fraction of a man.

Is the same happening? Am I setting myself up to suffer all over again? Maybe, but I don't think Peyton has a malicious bone in her body. I don't picture her hurting me on purpose.

As I step behind the bar, I approach Peyton like a scared animal. I plant each foot forward with care. Keep my frame relaxed and expression neutral.

The extended silence between us has run me ragged. Sleep has been shit. Two nights ago—when she sat in my living room and occupied my space—was the last time I ate. And the constant nausea has my throat raw.

I sidle up to her but leave inches between our arms. "Need help?"

She peers from the corner of her eye, then tucks her lips between her teeth. Just when I think she may say yes, she shakes her head. "I'm good. Thanks, though."

I don't want to walk away. Can't force my feet to move. "Ready for Monday? We can do one last walk through." At this point, I am throwing darts in the dark and hoping something sticks.

"No. Ani went over most of it with me." Of course she did.

"Well, if you need anything, I'm here."

Ugh. This fucking sucks.

I exit the bar without hurry. Send voiceless wishes to the universe Peyton will stop me as I head for the office. But my wishes go unanswered as I enter the hall and turn into the office. I drop into the chair, plant my elbows on the desk, and drop my head in my hands.

Only two days have passed, yet I don't know how much more of this I can take. Peyton's silence is a life sentence on death row. Years in solitary confinement with my arms in a straitjacket and soiled floors beneath my feet.

I swallow down my personal agony and bury myself in work. Distract myself with every possible task. Stay in the office until closing time and wallow in my new personal hell.

When Peyton and I go our separate ways at the end of the night, I say nothing. Not good night or goodbye. No "talk to you later" or "good luck on Monday." Nothing.

The worst part... she does the same. And after she drives out of the lot, I open my car door and spew the empty contents in my stomach across the concrete. No relief comes. Just the same emptiness I have felt since Thursday night.

I need to fix this. Fix us.

"What's up with you?" Gavin knocks me in the shoulder with his. "You've been scary quiet."

I am not in the mood to deal with questions or criticism. Life is shitty enough, no need to add another helping to the heaping pile. "Nothing," I grumble.

"Bullshit." I tilt my head to face Gavin and narrow my eyes. "We've known each other almost twenty years. Your lame, short answers don't fly with me, bro. You don't spill, I'll spew some bullshit to Shelly to make you talk."

Jesus fuck. Can a man not get one goddamn night without diving headfirst into the dark? All I want is one night. One. One night where Peyton doesn't own every other minute in my head. Is one night too much to ask?

Seems as if tonight will *not* be that night.

"Please don't."

"Then you better start talking."

This whole situation has repeated so many times in my head, new trails have been worn into my brain. Bone tired doesn't touch the fatigue in my muscles or the weariness in my bones. Each day moves in a blur as I go with the motions.

I flip into robot mode and reiterate the last week with Gavin. The good and bad. Moments I never wanted to end and the minutes that have yet to end. My best friend listens without interruption. Nods and winces and pinches his brows at all the appropriate times. Then he turns introspective as he processes it all.

"First things first. I'm on the same page as you." I scrunch my eyes. "Shit happens with condoms, but I wouldn't believe anything without proof. Sucks to think like that, but there's some crazy bitches in the world."

"Thank you." I take the first deep breath in days. "For days, I've felt like *I* was the asshole for being skeptical. Don't know how else to explain it other than saying *I just know*."

"Know what?" Shelly says as she steps into view and plops down on the lounger across from us.

Great. Obviously, we weren't *alone* in Jonas and Autumn's backyard. But I hoped Gavin and I would be able to finish this conversation without other ears or opinions in the mix. Looks like that isn't happening.

"Nothing," I mumble.

"Uh-uh." Shelly wags her finger in the air. "You don't get to be in some serious secret conversation with Gavin and not me. I'm your sister."

"Shell…" I hang my head. The second I tell her everything, she will rip me a new asshole. Guaranteed.

"What did you do, Micah?" Irritation laces her tone.

I lift my head and lock on to her familiar irises as mine glass over. Saliva floods my mouth as a boulder expands in my throat. I open my mouth, but nothing comes out. Gavin slaps my back when I don't say anything, then fills in the blanks for Shelly and the others lingering nearby.

"Told you not to hurt her." Her words are a growl on

her lips.

"Yeah, I remember. Not like I predict the future. And this… do you think I did this on purpose?"

"Of course not. But how did you not see this coming? You've probably banged over a hundred women in the last year. Did you expect *nothing* would happen except sex?" She crosses her arms over her chest and shakes her head. "If you say yes, you're dumber than I thought."

"Ouch, Shell. Tell me how you really feel."

"Maybe you need a reality slap, big brother."

"Well, consider me slapped. Punched is more like it, though. I know I fucked up. That's nothing new." I close my eyes, inhale deeply, then reopen them. "Now that we've discussed my shitty life, maybe you can help me fix it. Because…" I tip my head back and blink rapidly. Swallow, again and again. When I drop my eyes to meet Shelly's, hers glaze over too. "I don't know how. I fucked up and have been lost since."

Shelly hops up and comes to sit beside me. Her hands take mine and squeeze painfully tight. "Sorry I yelled." A tear rolls down her cheek, but she doesn't wipe it away. "But I knew messing things up with Peyton would be bad. Not just for her, but you too. You flaunt a hard exterior, but I know you, big brother."

Only around Shelly and close friends will I admit to being a softy. Not that there is anything wrong with not being a burly man twenty-four seven. That just isn't me. Hell, majority of the population walk around with phony fronts. Always splashing the best of the best. Do I want a good life with nice things? Sure. Who doesn't? But I don't give anyone a false sense of who I am. Have I made shitty decisions since Rochelle fucked me over? Definitely. Any self-respecting person would have lost their shit the same as me. Not everyone would fuck their feelings away, though.

"Shell, tell me what to do. She won't talk to me. She doesn't answer my texts. I'm trying to give her space. But if I give too much, will she walk away?"

I don't mean for Shelly to answer the last part, but she will. It's in her nature. In both of ours.

"Hate to say it, big brother, but you need to give her time." I drop my head in my hands and groan. Her hand finds my back and rubs the length of my spine. "In this instance, time sucks. But she needs to be able to form her own thoughts without you interfering. If you give it time, I'm sure she'll speak up sooner rather than later."

"This fucking sucks," I grumble against my palms.

"Yes, it does. What about this other woman?"

I straighten my spine, meet Shelly's gaze, and shake my head. "Told her to leave and not return without proof."

"How would she prove it's yours without DNA?"

"I meant that she's actually pregnant and can take a paternity test with me present." I close my eyes for three breaths. "Shell, I know my life has been out of control. That I have made such horrible choices. But I would never put myself in a situation like this. I have no plans to father children. At least not without being committed to someone and we both decide we want that."

She leans back and looks to the sky in deep thought. Her particular brand of silence is one I can handle because I know she's mulling over ideas.

Please let her have some solution to this.

Fatherhood may not be something I have given much thought, but if a paternity test proves—without a doubt— this woman is carrying my child, I will step up. I may not be ready to parent, but it doesn't mean I won't do my part. You do the deed, you take responsibility. Period.

"I have no absolute answers for you," she says with a pout, pushing out her lower lip. "But I'd suggest you quit fucking around, try not to worry over it until you have to, and just have patience." My eyes shut as I drop my head back to rest on the lounger. "Sorry, big brother. Not much else you can do at this point."

"Thanks, Shell," I whisper into the night.

She means well, I know this. But, fuck. I hoped she would say something—anything—that would lift me up. That would flip on the light bulb in my brain because I can't quite reach the cord. Her advice is solid. Just not what I want to hear.

What I really want is to text Peyton. To grovel and beg for her to talk to me. For her to tell me she needs time to herself, but she will be there in the end. Just some words to let me know all is not lost.

Because right now, all I feel is lost. I have never felt so alone and in the dark as I do now. Like I have no way out. Like each breath may be my last.

And I have no one to blame except myself.

FOUR

PEYTON

I HAVE NEVER HATED silence and distance. Not until now.

When one day bleeds into the next, when your mind never shuts off, gauging reality is a feat. And reality has been one gigantic blur since the woman in the red dress walked into Roar. Since I pretty much shut Micah out.

In the two weeks since she walked up to the bar and dropped the ticking time bomb, I have noticed a significant change in Micah. Not just physically, but also in his demeanor. With my new schedule, we see each other less. Which makes the changes that much more dramatic.

Across the club, I spot the purple crescent moons beneath his eyes. Notice the looseness of his shirt on his shoulders and chest, and the bagginess of his dress slacks. Every smile he flashes to the employees or guests is forced and brief. And he hasn't looked my direction in days. Too many days.

Seeing Micah like this, slowly sinking without a life preserver, wrings my insides to no end.

Is it the woman who has him gaunt and a shell of himself? Does the idea of becoming a parent scare him this much?

Our in-depth conversations prior to this never revolved around serious topics, such as marriage and children. Sure, we have both been in serious relationships and the idea of next steps may have crossed our minds. But obviously, ideas are where it ended since we are single and childless.

Or am I the reason for his frail frame and sullen disposition? Has my standoffish attitude and silence whittled him to this state? My eyes trail over his caved frame and dulled irises. Study his timid, forced smiles and the minimal energy he exerts with everyone—staff and patrons alike.

Micah and I share a horrid history, but we were headed in a new direction. To a positive place. A place full of second chances and possibilities, genuine affection and his lips on mine.

What if he hurts me? *What if he doesn't and this turns out to be what you've been waiting for?* The voice in my head has me backpedaling for the hundredth time in days. Has me seeing both sides of the coin. The same voice keeps me from making a sound decision. Because that voice belongs to my heart and it continues to argue with my brain.

"Making my rounds," I tell Mable as I exit the bar. Mable has been doing exceptional. Slaying Monday and

Tuesday with me and working Wednesday with more hands on deck.

I wander through Roar, doing my best to steer away from the karaoke stage setup in the middle of the dance floor. Out of the corner of my eye, Micah stays opposite me and heads for the hall. He lengthens his stride and his feet tread quicker. Before I fully turn my head to see him, he darts inside the office and closes the door.

Finishing my circuit around the club, I check in with the staff and patrons, then head to the office. Being away from Micah has given me time to think. More than enough time. At this rate, I am surprised my brain hasn't swollen or some form of self-combustion hasn't occurred with all my thinking.

But I am done thinking. Done seeing him suffer. Done asking myself questions I don't have answers to. Questions neither of us have answers to. Now, all that's left is us, suffering. And I hate it.

Although unnecessary, I knock on the door before turning the handle and entering. One, two, three steps into the room, Micah finally lifts his head from his hands. His starry eyes are puffy and lackluster and rip my heart to shreds. The dark marks beneath his lashes are more noticeable this close up. A vise squeezes my middle and holds me captive at what he has dealt with. Alone.

"Hey," I choke out and close the door without taking my eyes off his.

He licks, then tucks his lips between his teeth. His

head tilts slightly off-kilter as he breaks eye contact and stares down at the desk. "Hey," he says almost inaudibly.

I flip the lock on the door, then walk across the room. Wood scrapes concrete as I drag the guest chair around to park it beside Micah. He remains frozen as I sink into the chair and stare at his profile. Aside from the horrendous singing outside the room, silence consumes the space.

It eats me alive.

"Micah…" His breath stutters and, without second thought, I reach for his hand. "Please. Look at me."

Soft blond lashes dust his skin as his lids close. I give his hand a gentle squeeze and wait him out. Give him whatever time he needs. Life has changed so much—for us both—in the last two weeks.

Waiting, I focus on my breath. Count each inhale, each exhale. Concentrate on the warmth of his hand. The occasional callous where his fingers meet his palm. How his fingers twitch—just the slightest bit—every other heartbeat. And when his breathing calms, mine does too.

As if in slow motion, he tilts his head my direction. The muted-gold flecks over his dark-blue irises remind me of dying stars in distant galaxies. Their light fading and swallowing the darkness around them. Seeing them this close, seeing him this close, is a punch to the solar plexus.

Life-altering information was hurtled at him and I abandoned ship for my own selfish needs. I harbor no guilt for wanting to keep my heart safe. But I do foster guilt for not supporting him or lending an ear or shoulder. Especially when he needed me most.

"Sorry," I say, although the five-letter word doesn't feel adequate.

He laughs without humor. "Why are you sorry?"

My free hand comes to his cheek. Thumb brushes the arch of his cheekbone. Fingers comb through his hair. His eyes close as he leans into my touch. And the pang beneath my breastbone wanes slightly.

"Of all the times for me to go tight lipped, it's when you need my voice most. So, I'm sorry. For ignoring you and not being there when you probably needed me most."

He shakes his head and I drop my hand. His legs swing around and weave between mine as he scoots closer. "I did need you. But you needed space to think too." Fingers brush over my temple, down the angle of my jaw and to my chin. "Not gonna lie. Your silence, your distance, it sucked. But I respect it."

"Thank you."

His fingers continue to trace the ridges and valleys of my face. I close my eyes and bask in the trail of tingles his touch leaves behind.

"Missed you."

"Me, too." My eyes meet his with a list of questions, but I start off with a simple one first. "When's the last time you ate?" I probably sound like a nagging partner, but I don't care.

His momentary silence speaks volumes. "Haven't had much of an appetite. Been snacking here and there."

This jacks my guilt up to level ten. "Please eat." I grip

his biceps. "You've lost weight." Not in a healthy way either.

"I'll try." His thumb swipes slow over my bottom lip, his eyes following the movement. "Maybe we could hang after work. Make sure I eat." Doubt and hope lace his voice as he lifts his eyes to mine.

My first thought is to tell him yes. The last two weeks have been shitty. For both of us. But I don't want to give the impression that this is an easy fix. A supposed pregnancy won't just disappear. Not for weeks or months. But I also want to support him… and more.

"Can I think on it?" His gaze drops as he nods. "Let you know soon." I rise from the chair and bend to kiss his hair. "You do paperwork. I've got the floor."

After depositing the chair back in its place, I head for the door. Just as I reach for the knob, Micah's voice stops me. "Peyton?" The rough scrape of his voice fiercely hugs my heart.

I pinch my eyes for two breaths before peering at him over my shoulder. "Yeah?"

"Thank you." My brows scrunch. "Even if you don't say yes, this" —he gestures at the now vacant space beside him— "I needed it."

"Sorry it took me so long." I unlock the door and twist the knob. "Talk to you in a bit." And then I walk out.

Karaoke Night is in full swing. Beer pours from the taps and fruity cocktails fill fancy glasses. Laughter and cheers and the occasional perfectly tuned voice belts out over the sound system. Since we made the changes and

Ani has advertised the hell out of Monday through Thursday events, the bar has seen an uptick in guests and income.

After another circuit around the club, I help Mable and Kaylynn behind the bar. The next two hours bring interesting versions of Miley Cyrus's "Wrecking Ball" and Alanis Morissette's "You Oughta Know." The one to grab everyone's attention was the middle-aged woman dancing provocatively while singing Madonna's "Like A Virgin."

Yeah… I will never unsee that.

The crowd starts to thin as the evening wears on. Most people need to get home for decent sleep before work tomorrow. Mable and Kaylynn start cleaning up behind the bar and I help clean tables on the main floor. With the majority of the work done, I leave Charity to finish up while I check on Micah.

After a light knock, I enter the office. Micah sits studiously behind the desk, entering invoices. It takes him a minute to look up from the screen. But when he does, he rewards me with a smile I haven't seen in weeks.

Damn, I missed that smile.

"Almost done?" I ask.

"One more after this. Everything good on the floor?"

"Mmhm. Should be able to close on time."

The urge to laugh at our avoidance of whether or not we will meet after work takes center stage. I bite the inside of my cheek and resist.

"About after…" Micah, on the other hand, comes right out with it.

"I'll come over." Feet away, I catch the stars in his irises as they glimmer. Just from my agreement. Who knew Micah Reed's soft spot was the girl he picked on as a teenager? Certainly not me. "But only if food is involved."

"Bossy," he teases. That he jokes at all is a step in the right direction. "Think I like you bossy."

Well, that shifted quick. If the erratic thump beneath my sternum is any indication, I rather enjoy his response. I miss our banter. The constant teasing. And the way his eyes eat me alive.

I shrug a shoulder. "What can I say... I like taking charge."

"Hmm. You in charge sounds... fun." He licks his lower lip. "I'll order food as we leave and have it delivered."

Narrowing my eyes, I point a finger. "No weird shit."

"Says the woman who eats pineapple on her pizza."

"What's wrong with pineapple on pizza?"

"It's a fruit," he says as if that concludes the debate.

"Technically, tomatoes are fruit too. And you smear that shit all over the crust. So..." My lips pucker and brows lift. Let's hear your response now, fruit boy.

"Fine, I concede." I give him a snide smile and he sticks out his tongue. "And I promise nothing weird."

"Good." I start for the door and stop just as I step through. "I'll finish up out here. Then we can close up."

Before he answers, I head down the hall and back into the club. Most people have left and the few that linger appear to be finishing their drinks. Karaoke is being packed up as tables get shifted for tomorrow night's Bar Olympics.

The last of the stragglers leave and I lock the door. Mable, Charity, and Kaylynn wrap up the last of their closing duties and wish me good night as they head out the back together. The overhead and bar lights go black as I flip off switches. My heels clap down the hall as I head to the office.

Behind the desk, Micah scrolls on his cell phone and doesn't see me straight away. I lean against the doorframe and, for a moment, take him in.

The last two weeks have been rough, for him more so than me. Guilt still eats at me for ignoring him so long. But then I recall Reese and Aunt Leanne telling me to do what felt best for my well-being. If I wasn't strong enough to handle the situation, there was no way I could deal with it and stand strong beside Micah. I needed to work through some things in my own head. Decide whether or not it was possible for me to take this on. To date and stand beside a man who may or may not become a father to someone else's unborn child.

In the end, I changed my viewpoint. Looked at the entire scenario as an outsider.

Nowadays, people have children outside of wedlock all the time. Most of those people aren't in committed relationships. Some try a relationship for the sake of the child, but end up parting ways. Sometimes, what is best for the child isn't always the parents together. Especially if love doesn't exist between them. A forced relationship only adds more stress—for the parents and child.

This realization changed everything. Just wish it didn't take me so long to figure it out.

"Ready?"

Micah looks up from his phone. A soft, lopsided smile dons his face, and my heart rate spikes. God, I missed his smiles.

"Yep." He nods, taps the screen, then locks his phone. "Just ordered food. Should arrive about the same time as us." His voice is still scratchy, but less melancholy than hours ago.

I shuffle into the office and dig my purse from the desk drawer. "Perfect. 'Cause I'm starving."

Rising from the desk, Micah turns off the computer monitor. I flip off the light as we walk out. The trek to our cars is short, but filled with silence. A comfortable silence that has been missing between us for too many days.

"Drive safe." He leans in and I stop breathing as he presses his lips to my forehead. "See you at the house."

"'Kay." It's the only word I manage to get past my lips as he ambles to his truck. My heart squeezes a little tighter and I take it as a sign.

This may be the best thing—a relationship with Micah —to happen to me. Or I purchased my own one-way ticket to hell. Hopefully, it isn't the latter.

I scoop up the bag from the porch and punch in the front-door code. Peyton, less than a foot behind me, has my heart beating with purpose for the first time in weeks.

She's here. We are talking again.

Within hours, my life feels less daunting. All the craziness weighing me down — the possibility of fatherhood and an unhinged ex-bedmate — is pounds lighter now. Because Peyton is here. Her presence alone gives me a boost I didn't know I needed. Our relationship — the weird place between friendship and next level — may never be what it was pre–bomb drop, but Peyton approaching me tonight was a step in a favorable direction.

Over the last thirteen days, I had my doubts. Questioned whether she would speak to me again. With each passing day of silence and her obvious avoidance, I closed off more and more. Every time my phone alerted me to a text, excitement soared in my veins. Only to fizzle out a second later when I didn't see her name on the screen.

Work was worse. Ten times worse. Because of her promotion and the schedule changes, we spent less time in the same space. Her not stuck behind the bar all night changed things, too. Before her promotion, she stayed in one place all night. I could count on her proximity by stepping behind the bar. Could easily keep my eyes on her. But now, she is as mobile as me and almost impossible to pin down.

Until tonight.

Tonight, Peyton opened up to me again. Took initiative. Gave us another shot. And I won't waste the opportunity. Won't do anything to fuck this, us, up again.

We settle on the couch and I take containers out of the bag and set them on the table. "Hope you're good with Italian."

"Let me just get this out of the way." Shit. Does she have food allergies? I mean, she eats pizza. Practically devours it. Figured Italian was a safe bet. "I haven't met a food I *don't* like. Not yet, anyway."

Thank fuck.

"Good to know for future reference."

I open boxes to reveal cheese ravioli, meat lasagna, salad, and garlic knots. I hand her a paper plate and a package of plastic cutlery from the bag. We portion a little of everything onto our plates before scooting back on the couch, cross-legged, and digging in. Well, I eat a bit slower since my appetite was absent for too many days.

Last thing I need is to run to the bathroom and embarrass myself at the throne.

"Still working at the ALF?" I ask to spark some form of conversation. Although the quiet has been mostly comfortable with Peyton, I miss talking with her. More than expected.

"Mmhm," she mumbles around a bite of food. "Only on Sunday for a few hours, though." The corners of her mouth turn down slightly.

I love that Peyton is doing well for herself, but hate that her promotion has taken away something she enjoys. I may not know the entire backstory or understand her reasons, but working at the facility brings her joy. Spending time and chatting with a group of elders makes her smile. That is what matters.

"Sorry you don't get to visit as often."

"Thanks." The corners of her mouth tip up in a half-hearted smile. "Knew being there less would be a side effect to the promotion. Ms. Jenkins is happy with the change."

"Ms. Jenkins?"

"An older woman I visit with regularly. She's always telling me to move on and quit visiting the old folks. I tell her it makes me happy to see her."

"Does it?"

"Does it what?"

"Make you happy?"

Without an ounce of hesitation, she answers. "Yes. It's probably weird, but it reminds me of when I spent time with my Nana. She passed a few years back. I visited with her often. We talked for hours about my life and hers. She'd ask about my goals and how I'd accomplish them. I traveled the globe with her stories of adventure. On lazier days, we played cards or sewed cross stitch. Life with Nana was simple and peaceful and full of love. Every memory of or with her squeezes my heart." She places a hand over her heart and pats. In a blink, her eyes glass over and I see and feel every ounce of love Peyton had for this woman.

Her spending time at the facility makes more sense now. And I am more in awe of the woman beside me.

"Your Nana sounds like a wonderful woman."

"She was," she says with a sniffle.

"Sorry." Peyton scrunches her brow as she wipes under her eyes. "For upsetting you."

Peyton waves me off. "I love talking about her and reliving those memories. Please don't apologize."

"I'm sorry for two weeks ago. For what went down. I'm sorry it happened and you had the stress on your shoulders, too. I would never want that for you and it wasn't—isn't—fair."

"Not like you knew it would happen," she states.

"True. Still sorry. This whole ordeal shouldn't be yours to take on. Not the stress or concern. None of it. And I get why you needed time to sort through it all and how you felt."

Peyton jabs at her lasagna, her eyes darting left and right, then left again. When serious matters come up, I love that Peyton doesn't word vomit her feelings. She digests them and sorts through them before speaking her mind. She carefully crafts her words before opening her mouth. Because once out in the open, words can't be taken back.

"I didn't mean for it to take so long," she mumbles before lifting her gaze to mine.

A zing flares in my chest. My heart does a little dance, knowing she didn't want to be apart as long as we were. But the jubilation is quickly replaced with a pinch. I hate the melancholy in her voice, the slump in her shoulders, and the downturn of her lips.

Between the two of us, only I should be riddled with guilt. Not Peyton.

My knee grazes hers and I delight in the connection. "I know. But we all do things in our own way and time. Please, just don't shut me out again. I'll beg, if necessary. If you need space or time for yourself, just tell me. But check in from time to time."

Her eyes glaze over as she nibbles her lower lip. *Damn, I want my lips on hers*. Unhurried, she nods and frees her imprisoned lip.

"I will."

Unable to resist, I reach forward and brush the wetness off her cheek. "Please, don't cry." I lick the lone, salty tear from my finger. "Things were good between us. Then, my past barreled in and threw us in reverse." Closing my eyes, I inhale deeply, then meet the violet irises I have missed dearly. "And I'll understand if you want nothing more than friendship. For however long. I don't like the idea, but understand and respect it, if that's what you need."

Peyton stabs the middle of her lasagna with the plastic fork, then sets the plate on the table. Her fingers fidget in her lap. Her eyes downcast, watching the movement.

Why did I do this? Every good person or situation to enter my life… one way or another, I always fuck it up.

The few long-term relationships I had, Rochelle was the only person I envisioned a future with. A life beyond dinners, nights on the town, and sex. I had never fantasized about children or gray hairs. Just years—decades— spent loving each other.

The two women prior to Rochelle… the first wanted more when I wasn't ready. The second—we just grew apart. Both women were lovely, but never made me weak in the knees.

Early in my relationship with Rochelle, I felt that spark moment. The one where your heart flutters every time you think of the person. When your skin breaks out in a sweat seeing them. When your world wobbles a little because she is near. At the time, I thought fate was telling me she was the one.

Obviously, I was a gullible guy wearing rose-colored glasses.

Rochelle was my first real love. The woman who opened my eyes and heart to things I never knew. She was also my first heartbreak. The pain of her betrayal had nothing to do with the sex. It was more about my naivete and how someone I trusted completely stabbed me in the back.

I never wanted to experience pain like that again. Which led to my nighttime escapades. It was a way to vent my frustrations and fulfill my primal needs. Without getting attached. My philosophy—if I didn't form attachments, I would never suffer heartbreak again. Great philosophy for my mind. My heart didn't get the memo.

What I felt for Rochelle—during the best parts of our relationship—is nothing in comparison to what I feel for Peyton.

With Rochelle, my heart did this odd flutter. Nothing more.

With Peyton, my heart charges forward like an Olympian sprinter. Pound, pound, pounding in my chest. A fanatical swirl of energy sparks to life beneath my diaphragm. A passion that feels bigger than either of us. Powerful. Life altering. And more often than not, I forget how to breathe. Forget how to speak or function. My world doesn't just wobble with Peyton, it flips on its axis.

She may need us to dial it back a notch before jumping in the deep end. If so, I will understand and heed her wishes. I will tone down my feelings. A little. At least the emotions I put on display. The idea terrifies me, but I will do whatever it takes and keep my promises.

"Not that we titled our relationship weeks ago, but let's just call it friends," she says, voice shaky. An audible exhale leaves my lips as I sag deeper into the couch. "Until I mentally wrap myself around everything."

I should be grateful for any form of Peyton in my life. Not pouting like a petulant child. Hopefully, the shadow over my heart isn't flaunted on my sleeve.

"Long as I have you in some way, I'll call it a win. Thank you."

Friendship may not be what I want with Peyton, but time without her is out of the question. So, I take it and plan to do everything within my power to set things right. To show her I am not that guy anymore. That I am someone worth having as more than a friend. Not just a lover, but also a true companion. Someone she can rely and depend on. Someone she deserves and wants in her life.

We finish eating dinner and watch an episode of *Super-natural* on Netflix. With each passing minute, she inches closer to my side of the couch. Midway through the episode, she curls her legs under her butt and leans into my side. Head on my shoulder and hands clasping my bicep. Her breath warming the cotton of my T-shirt. Legs brushing my thigh.

If this is her definition of friendship, I take it tenfold.

When we evolve beyond friends again—because let's face facts, we will—I look forward to more cuddle time with Peyton. And what happens beyond first base.

Each time Peyton puts her lips on mine, she kisses me as if it will be the last time. Kisses me as if it's her dying wish. Full of heat and passion and frenzy. I only imagine what it will be like when I kiss her elsewhere. When I taste the saltiness of her skin and arousal on my tongue.

When I watch her come undone with my mouth alone. Or when she learns about my… accessories.

A wicked smile threatens and I bite my cheek. *Shift your focus, Reed*. Now is not the time to sport a hard-on.

All too soon, the episode ends. If it were up to me, I would let it roll right into the next. Keep Peyton curled up on my left. The last thing I want is for Peyton to leave. But bidding her good night is inevitable. For now.

"I should head home," she says and lifts her head from my shoulder.

Inch by inch, I trace a hand from her ankle to knee. When I reach the top, she shivers and the energy at my center swirls to life.

"Yeah. Okay." Although, what I want to say is *"no, don't go."*

Baby steps, again. Baby steps.

She starts picking up the trash from dinner, but I shoo her away. She puts her shoes on and I internally laugh at the pace. Slow. As. Fuck. Seems I am not the only one who doesn't want her to leave. My heart does a backflip.

Rising from the couch, we amble to the door. Those ten steps go far too quickly. Maybe it is time to rearrange furniture. Make the walk to the door twice as long. Who cares if it messes with the open space and feng shui. If it equals a few more seconds with Peyton, I am more than game.

"Thanks for dinner." Her violet irises closer to indigo when our gazes lock. She licks her lips and swallows. "Was nice being here again. Spending time together."

Unable to resist, I lift a hand and reach for the loose strands at her shoulder. She sucks in a breath. Her body freezes on the spot. I stare at the tendrils. How the indoor light accentuates her champagne locks differently than the morning sun. Study the natural wave that stands out enough to be noticeable.

I'd love to see her in a dress. Nothing fancy. Perhaps a sundress. Yellow, like daffodils. Hair down her back with more wave. Her bright smile across the table from me as we enjoy dinner by the water.

"Couldn't agree more," I say, voice scratchy.

Without warning, Peyton leans in and presses her lips to mine. The kiss innocent. Nothing more than a peck on the lips. But I don't dare move. Not to breathe. And certainly not to deepen it.

This kiss may be much tamer than previous ones we shared, but it is the most intimate yet. This kiss speaks volumes. Tells me she forgives me for my past discretions. Says she doesn't quite know how to do the friendship thing either. At least not with me.

Of all our kisses, this one is my favorite. This one, I will tuck away and keep safe.

Our lips break apart and she takes my hands in hers. "See you tomorrow." She spins and opens the door.

It takes a beat for me to notice Peyton is out the door and halfway to her car. I jog outside, down the steps, and catch up to her a second later. Her headlights flash before she opens the door and hops in. Once the engine purrs softly, she rolls down the window.

I want to kiss her again, but tell myself to stand down. Until she is ready for more than friendship, Peyton should initiate intimacy going forward. I won't ruin us. Not again.

"Drive safe." I tap the roof and reluctantly step back. "Tomorrow."

After a gentle smile and finger wave, she backs out and drives away. Watching her drive off sucks. But I was lucky to have had her here at all.

I press my fingers to my lips and smile. Until I see her again, the tingle her kiss left behind will remain on my lips.

SIX

PEYTON

WAS LAST NIGHT A MISTAKE?

I asked myself the same question for the umpteenth time since leaving Micah's house. The question distracted me the entire drive home. Cars and landmarks had passed in a blur. I vaguely remember saying good night to Reese as I zombie-walked to my bedroom. But the question kept me wide eyed in bed more hours than desirable. Woke me after maybe five hours of fitful sleep.

And now, as I lie in the comfort of my bed and stare at the ceiling, the question still haunts every synapses.

Was going to Micah's house and kissing him a mistake?

Over the last two weeks, I watched Micah morph into a shell of himself. Watched him turn into someone unrecognizable. More sullen. Frail. Lackluster. Each day, his posture slumped farther forward. The shadows under his eyes grew darker, more purple. And he refused to make eye contact with anyone longer than necessary.

Going to Micah's after work felt like the right thing to do when he asked. Agreeing to a friendship with him did too.

Then I blurred the lines less than an hour later. What a disaster I am.

I don't regret kissing Micah. Not one bit. I am, however, pissed at myself for sending mixed messages. If I say I want friendship, I shouldn't kiss him. Friends don't kiss. Well, not the way I kiss Micah.

"Damn it," I huff out as I slap a pillow over my face. Too bad smothering myself won't fix the situation. Too bad I don't know how to separate what I *should* do from what I actually feel.

Friendship with Micah is important and a major component of our relationship. Having a foundation—learning more about our backstories, what makes us tick, our individual mannerisms—matters. Doesn't need to be life altering facts. Small pieces build up. Like whether or not he picks his nose. Does he prefer the toilet paper over or under? Cats or dogs? Animal preference says a lot about a person. No matter, I don't want to enter a serious relationship without a history between us; even if the history is short.

Micah and I definitely have history. A path we navigated together and worked to improve. Then a tree snapped and fell over the path. Blocked us from moving forward. While Micah stood in front of the tree and tried to move it, I retreated. Stepped back into the brush and tucked myself away. Stayed hidden until comfortable enough to step into the light again. Now, we are back at the start. Trying to get around the tree and learning how to be a team again.

Starting over isn't easy. Not when you want to skip steps.

Hours had passed and I still feel the softness of Micah's lips on my lips. The scrape of his stubble along my chin. His taste on my tongue. It is too much and not enough.

A shiver rolls up my spine. A thin sheen of sweat blankets my skin. Heat blooms at the base of my tailbone and pools between my thighs.

"Ugh." I groan at how fast my thoughts went from point A to B. How I went from telling myself I need a friendship with Micah first to fantasizing about him. Am I a lost cause or what?

Peeling my arm away, I squint at the morning sunshine brightening the room. Sleep will have to wait. I throw back the covers and drop my arms in a huff.

Shower time.

Staying in bed any longer is not an option. My wayward thoughts are the last thing I need.

I make quick work of washing my hair and body. Then throw on lounge pants and a tank top. In the kitchen, I spy a folded paper on the counter. Unfolding it, I chuckle at Reese's scratchy script.

Morning Sunshine,
> *Stop laughing at my handwriting.*
> *Anyway… leftover breakfast casserole in the fridge.*
> *Xo*

I amble over to the fridge and retrieve the casserole dish. Scooping out enough for two, I plop the egg, sausage, and potato concoction on a plate, put it in the microwave, and press the two-minute button. I pour a tall glass of orange juice and toast a slice of bread while I wait. Settling at the breakfast bar, I eat and scroll through new emails, deleting the junk and scanning the keepers. Then I clear the other notifications. Same stuff, new day in social media land. No surprise.

After cleaning the dishes, I stretch out on the couch and distract myself with a few episodes of *Supernatural*. As the intro credits come to an end, my mind wanders to Micah. Until I suggested it, he had never seen the show. This seemed absurd. The show has fifteen seasons for crying out loud. As for me, I have rewatched the show. Not difficult when it is my "I don't have anything to do, so I'll watch TV" show. But Micah doesn't need to be privy to this information.

When the episode ends, I turn off the television and rise from the couch. "Lazy time is over," I mumble as I enter my room.

Since the promotion, I dress slightly less provocative

for work. My tops are still a bit snug with a dash of cleavage. But my bottoms are less second skin and more loose skinny dress pants. After wearing snug, curve flaunting pants for so long, dressing in looser attire has been an adjustment. The pants are growing on me more each day.

I twist left, then right as I check myself out in the full-length mirror. The yellow top has wide straps on the shoulders, forms a *V* at the start of my cleavage, flows over my breasts and hangs loose a few inches below the waistline of my black pants. The more I stare in the mirror, the more I evaluate myself. And the more I tell myself I look like a sunflower.

"Why is this so difficult?" I tug at the shirt hem. Contemplate switching out the top for a different color. "Ugh." I give up and stick with the yellow.

In the bathroom, I add enough makeup to be noticeable but not take an hour to apply. Brush my hair and opt to leave it down for once. Since I no longer dart like a madwoman behind the bar for nine-plus hours a night, I worry less about my hair in my face or drinks. Plus, not having my hair strangled in an elastic band all night is a nice change.

With my hair styled into soft waves, I exit the bathroom and slip on a pair of heeled boots. Grab my purse and phone, then head for the kitchen. I whip together a quick lunch, eat, then pack some snacks in my purse for later. One last trip to the bathroom, I lint brush my pants and swipe gloss over my lips before tucking the tube in my purse.

The sun beams down as I drive toward Tampa. Temperatures are too hot to ride with the windows down on the way to work. But I look forward to the salty wind in my hair on the drive home.

It isn't long before I park behind Roar, next to Micah's truck. How long has he been here?

I check the time on the dash—thirty minutes early. Either he arrived early to set up the rest of the Bar Olympics or in the hopes we would have more time alone. I have no qualms about spending time alone with Micah. But I am, on the other hand, still kicking myself for blurring the lines last night.

"Get it over with already," I coach myself as I exit the car.

Soft music echoes in the hall as I step through the employee door. I squint at the overhead lights as I reach the main floor. Scrunch my nose at the artificial lemon-scented cleaner in the air. I don't mind most cleaning product scents, but whoever decided this one was lemon is sorely mistaken.

I take a deep breath and enter the office. My brave face falls when I discover it is empty. I release my held breath and stow my purse in the desk drawer. Then I set off in search of Micah.

I exit the office, the click of my heels loud on the concrete. *Clap. Clap. Clap.* The sound thunderous compared to the music in the main room. The hall shrinks and my footsteps slow. At the end of the hall, I stop and scan every square foot of the club. It takes seconds to spot Micah.

Micah is across the room with his back aimed this way. He shuffles tables around and sets up the various games and events. Leaning on the wall, I observe him a moment. Take him in while his attention is elsewhere. Study the flex of his arms. Rake my eyes down his broad shoulders, defined back, and firm glutes. Call me piggish, but I want to enjoy this blip in time. To ogle the man without him giving me a ration of shit for doing so.

Then, I take a breath. Sooner than desirable, I shut the moment down and snap back to reality. Time to work.

"Hey," I say as I waltz in his direction.

He spins around, eyes me head to toe, and flashes me with the best smile. A smile I haven't seen in weeks. And I can't help but return it. Micah licks his bottom lip and I swallow.

"About finished with setup. If you want to lay out the beer pong cups." Micah points to a nearby banquet table.

I lay out the cups and set the balls in a bowl at each end. We don't fill the cups until people start playing. And the cups are changed out between each player rotation. Health code and all.

It isn't long before Roar fills with countless bodies. The deejay now takes requests on Thursday nights and plays upbeat music between those songs. Bar Olympics night—along with the other new themed days—has only been going for two weeks and already brings in a decent crowd. Roar easily makes double profits on Thursday nights since we changed it up. Adding fresh ideas was a smart business move for Ani and Sean. Each night continues to bring in new faces.

On the nights Micah and I both work, we trade off who gets paperwork duty. It eases me into my new role, but gives us the chance to not stare at a computer monitor and rows of numbers all night. The monotony of filling in spreadsheets, filing paperwork, writing schedules, and updating payroll doesn't bog me down. At times, I enjoy the simplicity and repetition. But hours later, my eyes grow weary. My mind a bit sluggish.

I tap Micah on the shoulder and he turns, giving me his starry gaze. A brilliant smile plumps his cheeks and brightens the room. And once again, I question whether or not kissing him last night was smart. Too late now. Turning back time only exists in fiction. Now, I just put one foot in front of the other and trek forward.

"I'm doing rounds, then going in the office."

Micah steps forward, stopping inches from me, close enough to touch without effort. And I forget how to breathe.

Son of a bitch. Breathe, Peyton. Deep breath in. Then exhale.

I inhale a deep breath, doing my damnedest to keep the action undetectable, and shuffle back an inch. But it's too late. The scent of his sweet cologne hits my nose and the room goes foggy. I beg my legs to move, my feet to carry me away from him, but nothing happens. My legs grow heavy and bury themselves deep in the earth like tree roots.

I am so screwed.

Perspiration slicks my skin and I send a silent prayer to the air conditioning gods, pleading for the cool air to kick on. Micah locks me in place with his magnetic eyes; the gold flecks sparkling with more intensity. I want to look away. I want to flee to the office and use the brick walls and industrial metal door as a barricade.

But I can't. Breaking eye contact feels impossible. A fool's errand.

Neither of us says a word, but I need space. And air. Air that doesn't smell of Micah and desire. I clear my throat and he blinks as if I woke him.

"I'm going to…" I circle my finger in the air and step around him.

One, two, three steps and I take a breath. A burst of cool air hits me, clears some of the Micah-induced fog, and allows me to think clearly. I take another breath and drop my shoulder, thinking I'm home free. Then a hand grips my bicep.

Without looking, I know whose hand is secured around my arm. Every sensory organ in my body alerts me to Micah's proximity. Even through the hate-filled years, I was aware of all things Micah Reed. Always.

I peek over my shoulder and flash my best work smile. "What's up?"

A tingle ripples from his touch down to my fingers and up my shoulder, neck, and chest. I conjure up any and every thought to distract me from the sensation. Public bathrooms, cottage cheese, scooping the litter box as a kid.

And it works... until his grip loosens and his fingers traipse down my bicep, my forearm, my wrist. Then he steps into me again. Invades every molecule of air within breathing distance.

Damn it. Damn it. Damn it.

Why must this be so difficult? Why am I torturing myself? For what?

It would be so easy. To take his hand in mine. Lace our fingers together and curl them tight. To feel the callouses on his warm skin as he strokes my thumb with the pad of his. To get lost in euphoria as sparks travel from my fingertips, my forearm, up and across my chest, to coil around my heart.

Believe me, I want to hold his hand. Want him so close, all I see and feel and breathe is him.

Should I, though? Let him invade me completely. Should I jump back in without reservation? My subconscious screams to slow down and use the time to learn more about Micah and the years we didn't know each other. Meanwhile, my heart beats erratically and begs me to cave. To give in to my desires; come what may.

Argh!

"Thank you," he says and steps closer.

My skin buzzes under his touch. God, I want to feel him everywhere. "For what?" I rasp, then swallow.

Get ahold of yourself, Peyton.

"Last night." A finger draws small circles over my pulse and I fight the urge to close my eyes. If he picks up on my galloping heart rate, he doesn't let on. "It may not have meant much to some, but it meant the world to me."

I will myself to respond. Tell my brain to part my lips and let the words flow freely. But nothing happens. My lips go on lockdown as I stare foolishly at Micah. When I manage to string words together, I sound like a bumbling idiot.

"Yeah. Sure. No problem."

What the hell is wrong with me?

Since when do I get tongue-tied around men? Around Micah? This isn't high school. A boy isn't asking me to a damn dance. I am an extroverted, grown-ass woman who doesn't take shit from anyone. My step has never faltered. Neither have my words.

Until recently.

One more circle on my wrist and Micah releases me. My skin prickles where we were joined. I want to wrap a hand or glove or bandage around the area. Trap the sensation so it will stay put. But I fight the urge.

"You look beautiful." The soft edges of his voice warm and soothe the wild organ beneath my breastbone. "See you in a bit," he says, then turns back to the bar and helps a waiting customer.

I shake off the daze that is Micah Reed and exit the bar alley.

Once I check in with the staff, I enter the office and lock the door. If I were the only manager on duty, the door would remain unlocked. But with us both here tonight, locking isn't an issue. Plus, I need solitude.

After catching up with the paperwork, I busy myself with straightening the office. Organizing drawers and tidying shelves. Rearranging the folder icons on the computer desktop and shifting furniture in the room. I do any possible thing to avoid exiting the office.

It sounds cruel—ignoring Micah—but I don't know what else to do. Last night, we agreed to friendship. But shortly thereafter, I kissed Micah. Jumped right over the friendship line. Possible presumptions were made. Thoughts strayed—at least mine did.

For now, I need this—us—to slow down. I need time to marinate in the idea of more with Micah. Again. Need time to consider how I might feel if Red Dress *is* pregnant.

I won't ghost him again. But with the weight of the situation hanging overhead, it only seems fair for me to be a little selfish. Right?

I scrunch up my nose and swat the air. Dust or a bug or hair tickles the tip of my nose. Pinching my eyes tighter, I rub the heel of my palm over my nose. As I drift back to sleep, whatever it is tickles my nose a third time. Bolting up in my bed, I flail my arms.

"Ow!" Reese belts out as I make contact with him.

My eyes fly open and I squint at the too-bright

sunlight coming through the blinds. Reese sits on the edge of my bed, rubbing his arm.

"What are you doing in here?" I groan out and fall back on the mattress.

"Well, I was trying to wake you up. Thought we could have breakfast out before my shift at the rec center."

I sit back up and stare at his faux wound. "Maybe you should wake me like a normal person. Nudge my shoulder. Call out my name." I purse my lips and lift a brow. "Not tickle my face and wait to get hit."

"Where's the fun in that?"

Throwing the covers off, I scoot out of bed and point to the door. "If you want to go out, I need to get dressed. Which means you need to exit, mister."

"Grumpy, sunshine."

"Yeah, yeah."

When the bedroom door clicks shut, I slump forward, press the heels of my hands to my eyes, and sigh. I love my best friend. Wouldn't want anyone else as a roommate. But sometimes, he really knows how to get under my skin. And laugh at my expense.

Fumbling through my dresser and closet, I go for easy and comfortable. It's early and I give no fucks about my appearance. Not after Reese woke me via tickle torture. Once my jeans are zipped, I drag a brush through my mane to tame the scary, then twist it up in a topknot. I slip on my black Vans, grab my phone and keys, and meet Reese in the kitchen.

Reese and I agree to take separate cars so he can go

straight to work after. We meet up at a local breakfast and brunch restaurant not far from the apartment. Thankfully, since most morning people have gone to work and it's the middle of the week, the place isn't jam-packed.

We get seated and order coffee while we peruse the menu. The server returns with a carafe and fills our mugs. Reese orders as if eating for two while I get biscuits and gravy with a side of hash browns and fruit.

With our orders scribbled down, the server takes our menus and wanders off. Silence stretches over the table as we fix our coffee how we like and take the first sip. No good conversation happens before this moment. At least not with me. I have no shame in admitting this.

"You sleep better?" Reese asks as he toys with the empty stevia packet.

I take another sip of coffee, then nod. "Yeah. Like a rock, actually."

"What changed?"

"Good question. Maybe it's all the office cleaning and rearranging I did last night to avoid Micah." I shrug a shoulder.

Reese's jaw tics as he glances out the window next to our table. "Thought things were better between you two," he growls, then meets my gaze.

"They are," I say in a rush. "It's just..." I pluck the creamers from the bowl and stack them into a pyramid to buy myself time.

"Just spit it out, Peyton."

"I may have confused him." After I stack the last creamer, I knock them down and start again.

"How so?"

The more I ponder this over, the more I question if I am overthinking the whole situation. Am I the only one focused on the fact I kissed Micah? Am I the only paranoid one reading too much into the moment? Probably. And also not surprising.

I stop stacking the creamers to look up at Reese, the corners of his mouth slightly upturned. His eyes bright as they stare back, as if he knows something I don't. *Feel free to share with the class, Mr. Triggs.*

"I told Micah I wanted to be friends again. Give things between us time, then go from there."

"Okay," he drawls out the word.

"I told him this two nights ago. And then I kissed him. More than once." I drop my head in my hands and groan. "Wasn't hot and heavy. But still…"

"Hey." Reese reaches across the table and jostles my arm. "Look at me." This feels like a parenting moment, one of those annoying times you get told what you did right and wrong. I don't want to look up, but I do. Reese lays his hand on the table, palm up, and I place mine on top. The warmth and slight curl of our fingers is a comfort I have only ever gotten from Reese. "You didn't do anything wrong. Can't help what you feel."

"Ugh. This sucks." He squeezes my hand. "I need things to slow down. Me kissing him counteracts the whole purpose."

"Why?"

"Why, what?"

"Why do you need things to slow down?"

My brows pinch at the middle as my head jerks back. "Are you serious?" Reese nods with the most somber expression on his face. "Did you forget what happened two weeks ago?"

"No. But I don't think Micah should be punished for something out of his hands and which may be false. Without proof, it's all hearsay."

Since when did my friend jump off the Peyton wagon and on the Micah train? Not cool.

"So, I'm supposed to forget it ever happened? Act as if his world is hunky dory and may not flip upside down in months? Seems idiotic, if you ask me."

Reese shifts his gaze out the window and loses focus. A few breaths pass and he gives my hand a light squeeze as his eyes drift back across the table. "What if all this stress you're taking on is for nothing? What if the woman isn't pregnant? And if she is, what if it isn't his? Then you put yourself through all this for nothing."

Does he not think I have considered this? God, I have thought over every possible scenario. Problem is, I have no clue which way to go or how to feel until the truth comes to light. I want to believe this outcome—that Micah has nothing to do with this woman's pregnancy. But I should also be mentally prepared for the possibility of it becoming a reality. And I need Reese to see both sides of the coin.

"What if she is and it is his? If I don't prepare myself for that, how will I cope? How will I know if I can have a relationship—in any capacity—with him? If I don't consider the possibilities of what our future may look like, how will I know?"

"Sunshine…" He sandwiches my hand between both of his as the most endearing expression touches his face. "There's no way to know what the future holds. But you impact it." I tilt my head and narrow my eyes. "If you constantly focus on the potential negative outcome, that's all you'll see and think." I open my mouth to rebut and he holds a hand up. "I'm not saying to discount the possibility. What I am saying is you shouldn't focus all your energy on the bad. If you like him, really like him, do what feels right *for you*. If that means time apart, so be it. But if it means time together, don't second-guess it." He leans down and kisses my hand. "Life is too short to miss out on the good. You of all people should understand this."

This is why I love and hate conversations with Reese. He tells me like it is and doesn't sugarcoat a damn word. And that last part… god, that hits home. Hard.

Far too often, I questioned if I'd ever find and hold on to love. Whether familial or romantic. Because the universe has thrown a lot of shitty cards for my hand. And it's difficult to believe anything else.

Reese releases my hand, sits back in his seat, and gives me time to process. To mull over what it is I want with Micah. To decide what steps I should take next. A decision only I can make.

Before I get too deep in thought, the server steps up to the table and delivers plate after plate. I unwrap my silverware, lean over my plate and inhale, and sag at the hearty scent of sausage gravy and fresh biscuits. Forks clink the ceramic plates as we eat in companionable silence. The entire time, I dissect everything Reese said. Take it apart, one word at a time, then restring it together to see if it makes better sense.

As his words cycle through my head for the hundredth, two questions pop up. Questions I need answers to, but fear what they will be.

Am I wrong to keep Micah at a distance? Or am I sheltering my heart so I don't lose someone else? Sadly, only I have the answers. If only I knew where they were hidden.

SEVEN

MICAH

WHY DID I agree to this? Why did I let Shelly talk me into coming here?

Naturally, Shelly is running late. Which is why I am still in my truck, with the engine and lights off, waiting for her arrival. Because I refuse to walk into the lioness's den without her. Okay, I may be exaggerating a bit. But after what Shelly said the other day, I can't muster the energy to enter my childhood home without her as a buffer.

So, while I wait, I stare at the only home my parents have owned. Picture perfect. I love everything about this house. All that it stands for and the love that resides in each square foot of the property. It irks me I haven't quite reached this comfortable stage as a homeowner yet. It's a marathon, not a sprint. Mom and Dad have worked their asses off for what they own. Have spent countless hours on every little detail, inside and out, to make their home shine. I remind myself of this each time I upgrade a room in the house or update the backyard and patio. All good things come with time. And patience.

Including love.

I stare at the two-story, natural brick home. The pristine white trim, decorative shutters and modern double front doors with large stainless fittings. Grass cut three inches tall. Hedges manicured and colorful flowers blooming along the front and down the walkway. Twin maple trees taller than the house rooted on either side of the long drive leading to the three-car garage. The house surrounded by an acre of land, an iron-and-brick fence and a gate.

The house wasn't always this gorgeous. All the hours and labor my parents have put in are an inspiration. It energizes me to take on the next project in my own home. Baby steps eventually lead to full strides.

Shelly pulls up and I breathe easier. We exit our vehicles and converge to walk to the house as a unit. We both love our parents, had a happy and healthy upbringing, but have zero excitement about tonight's dinner.

"You ready for this?" she asks.

"Not in the slightest. You?"

"No. Last thing I need is a reminder of my singledom. Or my lack of offspring."

Same. Although, if I play my hand right, I plan to not be single much longer. No comment on the offspring. But Mom and Dad won't be privy to either bit of news. Not yet. No need to have them barrage me with questions I can't answer. Nor do I want them to nag or ask to meet Peyton. Our relationship hasn't crossed that bridge yet.

Shelly opens the front door and leads the way. We toe off our shoes and set them on the rack past the foyer. Less than ten feet inside, the scent of pork, citrus, garlic and herbs wafts in the air. Soft jazz notes echo throughout the house. Mom says something about opening wine and I assume she talks to Dad.

We round the corner and spot our parents canoodling at the stove with their backs to us. Before we disturb the moment, I take it all in. How after thirty-five years of marriage—and seven years unmarried—they still hang on each other and kiss like teenagers. Dad has his arms locked around Mom's waist, her back to his front, as he whispers in her ear and she swats the air near him as she giggles. My heart swells seeing them so in love. The simple touches and secret conversations give me hope I will one day have a similar happiness.

"Hope we're not interrupting," Shelly pipes up as Dad kisses Mom's cheek.

They spin around, smile wide, and stop what they are doing to come hug us.

"How's my baby?" Mom asks as she wraps her arms around my neck. I circle my arms around her waist, lift her off the ground, and squeeze her.

"Good, Mom. Miss you."

When I set her down, she takes a step back and frames my face with her hands, eyes soft as she regards me. The lines on my forehead, the arch of my brow, the light in my eyes, the scruff on my jaw. "Miss you, too. Both of you." She peers over at Shelly, then swaps places with Dad.

"How's work been?" Dad asks as he hauls me to his chest and knocks the wind from my lungs.

"Good," I say once he releases me. "The owners have made some changes and it's been great for business."

"Like what?" Dad guides us farther into the kitchen, where he and Mom resume cooking.

I prattle off the new changes—leaving out all things Peyton-related. When I finish, Shelly looks at me like she did the one time I stole her clothes and towel from the bathroom forever ago.

"What?" I ask, scared of her answer.

"Why am I just learning about Karaoke Night?" Her brows shoot up and eyes widen.

Damn it. How the hell did I forget that my sister, Cora, and Jonas are karaoke buffs? Probably because I haven't hung out during the week with them in a while. After learning this new information, though, I bet I will see them Wednesday nights. Often.

I love my sister—and my friends—but seeing her at work feels a bit much. Maybe I am overanalyzing, but I like having time and a place that is just mine. Kind of.

"Uh…" Dad stands far enough behind Shelly she doesn't notice his *yikes* face. "Because I don't talk about work with you," I answer in staccato.

She rolls her eyes, then slaps a hand over her sternum. "Wound me, why don't you. If karaoke doesn't make you think of me, I feel like we need to bond more."

Oh, Jesus.

"Throwing it on a little thick there, Shell."

"What do you expect? My feelings are crushed." She play weeps and Dad bites his fist to resist laughing.

"Oh, please." I laugh and Dad joins in. "Work on your weeping skills, little sis."

"Alright, you two," Mom intercepts with hands on her hips. "Time to plate up and eat."

We line up beside the counter near the stove, grab a plate, and pile on the food. Mojo pork tenderloin, oven-roasted red potatoes, steamed green beans and homemade rolls. Needless to say, I put too much on my plate.

Mom and Dad lead busy work lives, but always make time for what matters. Family. Mom still works forty hours a week as a corporate marketing manager. She has the ability to retire in a few years without worrying, but she won't. That's what happens when you love what you do. Dad owns an insurance company that handles mostly vehicles, vessels and property. For a short time, he dipped his toes in the health and life side, but it became too taxing. Dad hit retirement age earlier this year, but said he plans to run the business a few more years before selling.

Both my parents have done so much in their career lives. They started at the bottom, put in their time, learned more about what they love, and worked hard for their career dreams. As a child, Dad often said, "Micah, you should never expect your dreams to be handed over. You have to put in the effort. Bust your butt until you get what you want. If you don't earn it, you won't respect it."

And I guess that applies to anything you want in life. Not just your career.

We sit in the same chairs we have since I was a child. Mom to my right, Dad on the left, and Shelly across from me. Dad fills glasses with sauvignon blanc while Mom lights the two candles in the table centerpiece. Nothing fancy. Just the norm.

Quiet consumes the first few minutes around the table as we taste the meal. I sample a little of each before the silence is broken.

"Excellent as always, Nicole."

"Agreed," I follow after Dad. "Really wish I had your cooking skills, Mom."

Mom eyes Dad across the table as her cheeks pink. "Thank you." Eyes that mirror mine shift my direction after breaking contact with Dad. "And you, too." She cuts and pierces a piece of pork loin. "We can try cooking lessons again. If you want."

One trait I love about Mom… she never gives up. I may burn or undercook every dish I attempt, but Mom still holds on to hope. I love how she feels I am not a lost cause.

"Maybe." I reach over and rub her forearm. "Might be best to start with recipes written for kids, though."

The entire table erupts in laughter. Years have passed since I cared whether or not I got teased in the cooking department. Can't be good at everything. May as well own it.

"I'd love that, Micah. Let me dig up some recipes and we'll plan a day to get together."

"Sounds great, Mom."

So far, tonight has gone smooth. Shelly had me frazzled for days. Worried about conversations over relationships and grandchildren. But the night has been normal. Good food, smiles and laughter. Everything I love about my parents and where we grew up. Couldn't be more perfect.

"Shelly," Dad starts and she turns to face him. "Still seeing that nice young man from the Italian market?"

And… I jinxed us.

Thank goodness she swallowed her bite before he finished speaking. Her eyes flit to mine and beg for help. But I have nothing. The second I come to her defense, Mom will jump on me with a similar question. Then we will both sweat under the spotlight. Better to let her go first, then I will follow. Cruel, yes. But that's what older siblings do.

Shelly stabs a potato with pent-up aggression. "No, Dad. We went on one date and I felt really uncomfortable." I widen my eyes at her and she shrugs. "He didn't *do* anything wrong. Just a vibe."

Dad takes her hand and consoles her. "Never be upset for turning down someone who makes you uneasy. I will always be in your corner. You mean the world to us, Shelly Bear."

"Same," I say. Speaking up and agreeing with Dad is

right. I will always be there for my sister and family. In a heartbeat. And they will do the same.

The seriousness of the moment fades and we all breathe easier. Then, Mom shifts her attention toward me and whips out her inquisition claws. *Damn it.*

"What about you, Micah? Is there a special lady in your life we should know about?"

Why? Why did I agree to this? And why are our parents pestering us about our romance lives? Well, lack of romance.

What spurred this on? Dad had his annual birthday checkup with Doctor Harris not long ago. Hopefully, it all went well and this isn't Mom and Dad's way of saying they don't have much time left. I don't enjoy their nosiness, but I would take it over bad health any day of the week.

"No, Mom. Can't seem to nail down the right one." Which is not a lie. Mom just won't hear my words how I mean them.

We all quiet and go back to eating. I chew the pork and potatoes way longer than necessary. Keep my mouth busy in case one of my parents decides to pry further. I pray the relationship talk will stay where it is. In the past. And once again, I should quit thinking. It's as if Mom or Dad have a sixth sense, as if they hear my every thought or pick up on the exact vibe of my mood.

"With the massive population in the area and technology, I figured my kids would've married by now," Mom mutters before biting her roll.

Why didn't I put a contingency plan in place? Should have asked Gavin to text or call. He does owe me a favor, after all. Or have Cora do the same with Shelly. Both of us came here knowing our parents were on a mission. To marry us off and make us baby factories. Not really, but that is how it feels under the current spotlight.

Part of me wants to counter Mom's comment. But if I open my mouth, it will fuel the fire. So, I bite my tongue. My sister, on the other hand, didn't get the memo to keep her mouth shut.

"You'd think with the massive population and all the dating apps, there wouldn't be thousands of creepy guys in the area." Shelly shrugs, then stabs the pork loin on her plate with pent-up anger. *Shit.* "But most only want one thing. And it isn't commitment." She shovels the bite in her mouth and doesn't look up.

My blood boils that Shelly feels the need to defend herself like this. Especially to our parents. Are they aware of her lack of sexual experience? Doubtful. If they were, there is no way they'd be so eager to push her into the arms of a random guy. All for some picture-perfect idea they have in their heads.

"Surely, they're not all bad."

That's it. Conversation over. "Mom!" I bark out. Her fork freezes halfway to her mouth. "Drop it."

"Micah, don't speak to your mother with that tone."

My eyes dart to Dad. "Don't mean to be cruel. But this conversation… it's uncomfortable. For both of us."

"Sorry, sweetheart." Mom rubs Shelly's forearm. "Just

don't want either of you to miss out on the opportunity to have a family of your own."

I turn back to Mom, softening my tone as I speak. "I get it. But have you given thought as to *why* we aren't with someone? Sure, I could stay with a random hookup—"

"Micah," Dad grumbles.

"No, Dad. Hear me out." I set my fork down, wipe my mouth, and fold my arms across my chest. "Is it so wrong for Shelly to be picky? Shouldn't she wait for the guy—or girl—that makes her happy? She has her own reasons for being single." Shelly's eyes widen. "Which are none of our business unless she wants to share."

"Okay, we're sorry," Dad says with sincerity. "Hope you understand this conversation came from a place of love." He and Mom look at each other, then us.

"We do," I answer. "And as soon as either of us wants to introduce someone, we will. So, please, can we not bring this up again?"

Mom scoots potatoes around her plate, her eyes following the motion. Dad does the same with the last of his green beans. *Jesus*. They act like pouty children. I love my parents, always, but this is ridiculous.

Chair legs scrape the wood floor as I rise and grab my plate and head for the kitchen. I scrape the last of my food into the trash, rinse the plate and put it in the dishwasher. I drag my fingers through my hair and tug.

Shelly prepped me for what was coming tonight, but I had no idea it would set me off. Not like this. I don't typically lash out at my parents. Tonight, though, feels different. The weight, the pressure... an expectation I have never dealt with from them fists my heart in painful ways.

And I don't know how to handle it.

"Micah?" Mom calls out, her voice soft as she approaches.

"In the kitchen."

She rounds the corner, sets her plate on the counter, walks straight to me and wraps her arms around my waist. My arms wrap around her waist as I haul her closer and rest my cheek on her head.

"Sorry," she mumbles against my chest.

I rub a hand up and down her back. "It's fine, Mom. Just please, respect our choices. And privacy. We'll tell you when the time comes. Promise."

She drops her arms and steps back. "Okay." Matching eyes hold mine as a gentle smile curves up her lips. "Just want you both happy."

Shelly and Dad shuffle into the kitchen and clean their plates. The thorny topic gets dropped and we dish out dessert—mixed berries and chocolate cake with fresh whipped cream. Shelly and I hang out a while longer once our plates empty. Fortunately, everyone but me has to be up in the morning. So, the evening ends early.

Hugs are exchanged on the front porch as Shelly and I step out to leave. Mom says she will reach out to us both for the next get-together.

On the way to our cars, Shelly mutters, "Thanks for the save earlier."

I bump her shoulder with my arm. "Always, little sis. They mean well, but their persistence frustrated me."

"Yeah, I picked up on that." She chuckles as we reach her car and she opens the door. "Remind me to never pester you."

"Whatever." I play shove her in the car. "Drive safe. Love you."

She blows me a kiss. "Love you, too, big brother. Talk to you later."

I drain the last of my beer. The *Peaky Blinders* episode ends and I shut off the television. Silence engulfs me as I turn off lights, close blinds and curtains, and check the door locks.

The short distance to my bedroom is a mile long tonight. My usual solace with solitude has taken a back seat.

I strip my clothes, toss them in the hamper, pull back the bedding and slip under the covers. For a moment, I lie in the dark with an arm tossed over my eyes. Take a few breaths as all the relationship talk filters back in from earlier tonight.

My parents mean well, but don't grasp the example they set for us. Shelly and I will never just settle. Not for some random person who we check *some* boxes off with.

No, whoever we choose will have to check off all the boxes. Will have to fill all the cracks and seal old wounds. Make us see the world with new eyes. Make us *feel.*

We aren't emotionless people, but Shelly and I don't give away love freely. And letting someone new get close is a feat. Years ago, I let people in easier. Loved more openly with family, friends, and romantic interests. Then Rochelle fucked me over and my trust in the opposite sex fizzled. At least when it came to love.

Until Peyton.

I slap a hand in the direction of the nightstand and locate my phone. Tapping the screen, the background lights up. A picture of me and Shelly smiles back at me from my birthday this year. I unlock the phone, open the message app, and tap on Peyton's name.

Too many days have passed since we texted back and forth. As of recent, the texts have been one sided. From me. She needs time, I get it. But I reject the idea of leaving her alone altogether. Out of sight and all that.

Before the idea dies, I type out a message to her and hit send.

Micah: Awkward dinner with the parents tonight 🙄 You'd think that'd end when you're an adult.

I lock the screen, lay the phone on my stomach and stare at the wall. The shadows from the oak tree and streetlight dance over the cream-painted wall opposite my bed. Leaves flutter on the branches and I try to create other shapes out of their combined shadows.

I jolt when my phone vibrates. Fumble as it slides off my chest and hits the sheet. Scramble until I locate and unlock it.

Peyton: Probably wasn't intentional.

For a moment, I stare at the screen and forget to breathe. *She answered.* That has to mean something. Right? Probably best to not read into it too much. Not yet, anyway.

Micah: Nah. They want us happy, but approached it all wrong.
Peyton: What happened?

I scoot closer to the headboard, toss the second pillow on the one under my head, and inch upright.

Micah: Asked if either of us is dating. They're worried we'll miss out.
Peyton: What'd you say?

Her response makes me smile. I may read into it more than intended, but it seems she wants to know if I told my parents I was dating someone.

Micah: That when either of us wants them to meet

someone, they will. It got a little heated. Which isn't normal.

Peyton: Sorry you had a crazy night.

Micah: Thanks. Better now.

Peyton: Is that so?

I read the last text with her voice in my head, imagining her hands on her hips and brow perked up. *Fuck*. How I miss this side of her. The snark and banter and sass. The side that has me crawling like a bumbling fool.

Micah: Damn straight.

Peyton: And why is that?

Micah: Hmm 😑 Maybe because a certain someone is awake.

Peyton: Do you have a pet?

God, she makes me laugh. Lifts away the heavy and provides incomparable comfort.

Micah: No. Do you?

Peyton: No, but I want a cat.

Micah: Good to know.

Peyton: Are you allergic?

Micah: No. But it's always good to know the competition.

For the next hour, we text back and forth. Talk about randomness. Some with substance, but not much. By the time we say good night, a peculiar bouncy sensation ping-pongs beneath my rib cage. I press the heel of my palm to my sternum, take a deep breath, hold it until my lungs burn and relish in the bliss Peyton delivers.

I have no clue what this is between us. But I plan to do whatever it takes to keep it. To keep her. Who knows… maybe in the not-too-distant future, I will have dinner with my parents and tell them about Peyton. Introduce her to them. One day…

EIGHT
PEYTON

How do so many people know this much random shit?

When I first suggested Trivia Night to Ani, I figured it would revolve around movies, television and basic geography. Questions like "what is the capital of Arkansas?" or "name the show with a woman who performed magic with a twitch of her nose." or "who crushed on Penny first in *The Big Bang Theory?*"

What we got instead was some serious nerd action. Super. Nerd. Action. And it's kind of hot. I never pictured myself interested in highly intelligent men—the nerds of my youth were... odd—but I have a newfound appreciation for them. The women too.

"What's the diameter of Earth?" the trivialist asks.

Bzz.

"It's 7,917.5 miles," Mr. Rolled Sleeves answers.

"Name the largest sea on Earth."

Bzz.

"Philippine Sea," Mr. Tall and Lanky states.

"List three Wonders of the Ancient World."

Bzz.

"Great Pyramid of Giza, Hanging Gardens of Babylon, Lighthouse of Alexandria," Ms. Hot Librarian says as she straightens her spine and pushes glasses up her nose.

Gina sidles up to me and fans herself with a coaster. "Damn."

Tipping my head back, I laugh. "You and me both, girl. Never saw this day coming." She lifts a brow. "When intelligence ranks in the top three traits to tick off." At this, Gina laughs with a shake of her head.

"Speaking of guys…"

Over the last six weeks, since my promotion, Gina and I have bonded. We aren't to the point where we hang outside Roar. But it has been nice forming this new relationship. Having another woman to shoot the shit with. Someone I can vent with or tell dirty details to.

She hadn't been blind to the chemistry between me and Micah. Neither has most of the staff. My stomach constricted when she let me in on this non-secret. Guess I had been willfully blind to the staff and everyone else setting foot in Roar. Now, I notice every little detail. Pay attention to the way they watch us on the nights we work together. Pray our interactions don't disrupt work.

Because things between Micah and I could definitely disrupt.

"Yes?"

Pulling down on the tap, Gina fills a pint glass and

hands it to a shorter man with shaggy brown hair. He scurries back to his chair, sips the beer, and holds his hand over his buzzer. This crowd stirs the best belly laughter and intriguing inquisition. Trivia Night was one of the best ideas, hands down.

Hands on her hips, mouth in a firm, straight line, Gina shakes her head. "Don't play coy."

I put on my best poker face while I laugh internally. *But it's fun.* "Well" —I wipe the bar— "you didn't ask a question."

A sharp sting bites my skin after Gina whacks my bicep with a bar towel. "Smart-ass." Rubbing away the sting, I shrug. "How's things with starlight?"

Gina has no idea why I call Micah starlight. One night, she overheard us talking and my casual use of the nickname. Since then, she throws it out on occasion when we chat. I have no intention of telling her the meaning behind the name. All that would do is add another twenty questions to her mile-long list. For now, she believes it's just me teasing him. I have no intention of changing her opinion.

"Good."

With Gina, I give vague answers. One—it drives her crazy. Two—I don't feel the need to divulge my entire life. Our friendship fairly new, I choose to keep some parts of my life private. Only one friend gets all the dirty details. Reese. Our bond wasn't always what it is today, but we have been tight for years.

"Good?" she deadpans.

"Yeah. Good."

"Remind me to never ask you for detailed opinions in the future."

I laugh and mix drinks for an order Charity drops at the bar. "You got it." Setting the Jack and Coke, Cosmo and IPA on the tray, Charity flashes her award-winning smile, then walks off to deliver the drinks. "Things have been good," I say once Charity is out of earshot.

The staff may be aware Micah and I are friends — or more than friends, no definitions have been laid out. I don't make a point to ask their opinion. What Micah and I have should not interfere with Roar. All workplaces are different — some lenient on personal relationships outside work, others not so much. Seeing as Ani is a friend and I tell her quite a bit, she is cool with whatever Micah and I have, so long as it doesn't interrupt business.

For the most part, we maintain our managerial persona when on the floor. Sporadic flirting and banter are good for business. What we do away from the crowd is a different story.

Things with Micah haven't veered back to steamy kisses and hands under shirts. Yet. But we seem to be speed walking the same path that led us there before. Part of me jumps at the idea of kissing Micah again. Ready to feel his soft, warm lips pressed to mine. Taste his hunger on my tongue. Thinking about it makes my mouth water and thighs clench.

My phone vibrates in my back pocket and I snap out of my wayward thoughts. Slipping it from my pocket, I glance down at the notification and snort. Micah's ears must have been ringing.

"What's funny?"

"Micah." I shake the phone in my hand. "Like he knew we were talking about him."

"Creepy." Gina wanders down the bar, chats with customers not playing trivia, and leaves me to read the text in privacy.

Micah: Come over tonight 🙏

In the last month, Micah and I have hung out after work more. Gone to Teddy's on occasion, but spent more time in his living room with take-out boxes and episodes of *Supernatural*. Last week, he introduced me to *Peaky Blinders*. Although he watched three of the seasons, he swears starting over is fine.

Peyton: I don't know. These trivia guys are kind of hot.
Micah: You want to play twenty questions, hellcat?

I bite my lower lip and fight the grin begging to come out. I spin to face the wall of liquor bottles and hide the heat on my cheeks. Don't know what it is, but the nickname he gave me makes me hot, bothered and goofy.

Peyton: Depends…
Micah: On?
Peyton: Mood. Food. Booze.

Why did I press send? It isn't only my brain that forgets how to properly function around Micah Reed. Obviously, my fingers have a mind of their own as well. *Swell.*

Micah: Really?
Peyton: Yep.
Micah: Best get your ass here after you say good night to the trivia BOYS.

I laugh out loud and Gina shoots me a *that good, huh?* With a shake of my head, I wave her off and resume texting.

Peyton: They are definitely MEN. Who knew nerds this good-looking existed?

Now, this is fun. Something about banter with Micah makes my chest lighter. Tugs at the corners of my lips. Makes my heart stutter. My breathing stammer. I dish it out and he gives it right back. It's who we are, only the context has morphed over the last two months.

Micah: You want nerdy?
Peyton: I mean…
Micah: Be here after work 🤓

The urge to drag this out further tempts me, but I cut the conversation short. If I head into the office, paperwork will occupy me long enough for the night to end soon.

Peyton: I like it when you're bossy 😌 Later.

I stow my phone in my pocket and ignore the final buzz. Passing Gina, I signal toward the office and she nods. Behind the closed door, I slump down in the desk chair and eye the stack of work. Most of it is menial, but necessary. Never expected to be a number cruncher. Someone who sits behind a desk and fills in spreadsheets. But here I am, squeezing the armrests on the chair while tucking myself closer.

And I love it.

NINE

MICAH

I READ the last text I sent for the tenth time.

Micah: You haven't seen bossy yet 🙄

She hasn't opened the text, but she will once work wraps up.

My connection with Peyton over the last month has been this force. Gradual yet powerful. Strong yet gentle.

After the night we agreed to give friendship another try—let's not forget the kiss, I sure as hell won't—our relationship has bloomed. Neither of us has titled the relationship beyond friendship. Yet. But the chaste kisses from week one have morphed into longer kisses and frequent caresses. No suck-your-soul kisses or groping of parts, but my crystal ball indicates we are headed that direction.

I order pizza online and schedule it to be delivered around the time she typically arrives. Then I surf through movie options. Usually, we watch an episode or two of my show or hers. But after her snarky comments earlier, a change of plans seems in order.

After I choose the movie, I peel off my shirt on the way to the bathroom. Ditching the last of my clothes, I crank the shower and step under the hot spray. I wash up in record time, towel off, and sort through my wardrobe for the perfect attire.

I wander from the bedroom into the kitchen and dig out the candle lighter and jar candles. Next time I see Shelly, I must thank her for the obscene number of candles she gifted me over the years. Most of them have been decorative dust collectors for years strategically placed in the main space of the house.

Tonight, though, they will be put to good use.

After I light enough candles to heat the house, I stow the lighter, then grab a bottle of wine from the fridge. I pop the cork, set the bottle on the counter, and let it breathe.

Mood. *Check*.

Booze. *Check*.

And any minute… the doorbell chimes. "Food."

I open the door and am greeted by a smiley young man that hands me two large boxes and a bag. The moment he exits the porch, Peyton parks in the driveway. She cuts the ignition, hops out, and practically skips to the front door.

Fuck, she's adorable.

"Hey," Peyton singsongs as she openly ogles me. "Look at—" She freezes as she takes in the main room of the house. "What's this?" Spinning around, a crease forms between her brows.

"Mood, booze" —I set the pizza, salad and garlic bread on the counter— "and food."

"And this?" Peyton lays her palms beneath my collarbones, then, inch by inch, drags her hands down my abdomen. Her thumbs brushing the column of buttons.

"Going for the nerdy look." She lifts a brow. "Didn't find the fake glasses before you arrived."

Her arms sweep around my waist and rest on my lower back. "You don't need them."

Hands on her hips, I secure Peyton in my grip. If I leaned forward an inch, her lips would be under mine. But anticipation is everything. And I love the push and pull between us.

I lean in and she gasps. Instead of kissing her, I brush my cheek along hers and stop at her ear. "Time to eat," I whisper, then nip her lobe. Her body shudders beneath me and the corner of my mouth twitches. My fingers drift along the inside of her forearm and lace with her fingers. "C'mon."

I guide her to the couch, park her in the spot I dubbed hers and go back to grab the food, wine and glasses. Everything on the coffee table, I sort the boxes while she pours the wine. I turn on the television and hit play on the movie as we dig in.

"Really?" Peyton asks on a laugh-squeal as the intro of *The Princess Bride* pops on the screen.

"What? It's a classic."

"Never pegged you as someone to watch *The Princess Bride*. That's all."

"Well…" I cock a brow at her. "I'm full of surprises."

The movie starts and we settle back on the couch, cross-legged, with salad and pizza in our laps. For a bit, we focus on the movie and dinner. Several years have passed since I last watched this movie and I forgot its greatness.

Around the time when Iñigo talks with Westley about the six-fingered man, Peyton leans forward to set her box on the table. Her knee brushes mine in the process. And when she sits back with her wine, her leg presses and remains butted to my thigh. The motion natural, leisure. As if it wouldn't be any other way.

And I no longer want to hold back. No longer want to resist the one person I want. Her.

I set my box on the table, reach for her glass and put it down. "Hey," she contests.

But before she gets another word in, I lean back, twist in place, frame her face in my hands and bring my lips to hers. She freezes for one, two… then her lips move with mine, soft and sweet at first as her hands snake behind my neck. It isn't long before her lips part and she sucks on my lower lip. She tastes of tangy grapes and herbs and something distinctly Peyton.

My hands drop from her face to her hips as a growl

rips from my throat. Her fingers trail into my hair and fist the strands.

Fuck. She will unman me on this couch.

As the thought takes residence, she shifts and slowly lays back, bringing me down with her. I hover inches above her, my arms framing her face and weight pinned between her thighs. Our lips and tongues dance in sync as we give in to the desires we stowed for too long. Her back bows off the cushion and her breasts press to my pecs as she rubs my dick with her pelvic bone.

God, she is fucking perfect.

My hand skims down her shoulder, along the curve of her breast, and she pushes into my touch. I continue my venture down her torso, graze her abdomen, and slip my fingers under the edge of her top. The heat from her skin ripples up my arm and undulates across my chest. Jolts my heart. Expands my lungs. Gives me life.

A hand trails down my back to my elbow. Her fingers drift down my forearm to my wrist and rest on my hand. I am ready for her to stop me, us, from taking this moment any further. Our mouths continue their assault, my hand still on her skin. What I don't expect is what happens next. Peyton guides my hand up her body. Skin to skin, my fingers float over her abdomen, her stomach, her lacy bra cup.

A moan spills from her lips and I swallow every thrum. The resonance vibrates against my palm. Drives me wild. Urges me further.

I shove her top up, tug it over her head, and toss it to

the floor. Dropping down, I kiss the spot beneath her ear while I unhook her bra from behind. Peeling the lacy fabric off, I take in her bare breasts for three jagged breaths. Not too big nor too small. Dark-pink areolae with pert nipples in the center. "Perfection."

My mouth crashes down on her lips with another vicious kiss. My hand palms her breast while I twist the nipple between my thumb and forefinger. She rocks her pelvis and rubs my cock with flawless precision. I snake a hand around the back of her neck, comb my fingers through her hair, fist the strands and yank her head back.

Her gasp breaks the kiss and I trail my lips down the front of her throat, past the hollow and between her breasts. Lick my way left, suck the stiff bud between my lips, add a little teeth.

"Micah," she breathes out. "Fuck."

"You like that?" I ask and circle her nipple with my tongue.

"God, yes."

I pay equal attention to her right nipple. Peyton claws at my scalp, tugs my hair, mewls as I lick my way down, down, down her abdomen. When I reach the hemline of her pants, I lift my gaze to meet hers and ask permission.

"Yes," she says, breathy.

My lips drop back to her belly, kiss her sweet flesh, lick her navel. I unbutton her pants and tug down the zipper. I sit up, scoot back and drag the fabric down her thighs, her calves, then drop them on the floor. As badly as

I want to rip her panties off, I leave them in place. For now.

"So fucking perfect."

I lift her leg, drop her ankle on my shoulder and kiss the lower inside of her calf. Drag my fingers up the length of her leg as I lick a trail up the inside of her knee, her thigh. Mid-thigh, I suck the skin there. One hand at her hip. The other trails up her belly to her breast and pinches the nipple.

Peyton claws at my shirt. Tears at the buttons. Rips the fabric apart and sends buttons skittering across the room.

"I want your skin on mine."

Hooking her leg on my hip, I wrench the shirt off and toss it behind me. Drop my weight over her, crush my lips to hers, smash her breasts with my chest, and grind the bulge in my pants against her apex.

My hand snakes around her backside, my fingers trailing up her spine. Peyton lined up with my body… damn, this woman was built with me in mind. The lines of her neck and swell of her breasts. The planes of her abdomen and angles of her hip bones. How her lips move in synergy with mine. Her tongue dances the same familiar tune with mine.

Peyton and me, we are perfection.

I clutch the back of her neck, break the kiss, and make the trek back down her body. Taste the saltiness of her skin as I trail down her breastbone, her abdomen. Inhale her coconut mint scent with each new area of skin my lips touch. Trace the soft flesh along the outside of her thigh with my fingers as I drop low, low, lower.

Peppering kisses on her lower abdomen, I peer up at her and lick along the low hemline of her panties. She fists my hair and shoves me lower.

"Something you want?" I mumble over the thin strip of fabric separating her skin from my lips.

"Teasing time is over."

I blow gently over the apex of her thighs and she trembles. "Is it, though?"

She props herself up on an elbow, clutches my chin and tips my eyes to hers. Her violet irises glow with hunger and I swallow. For a beat, her eyes drop to my lips as she licks hers.

"Taste me," she moans out before dropping her hand and shoving my face between her legs.

Jesus fucking Christ.

Until both of us are bone tired, I do exactly that. Taste her. Give her one orgasm after another. Torture her in the best possible ways. And when she offers to return the favor, I decline. At least for tonight.

Peyton needs to know I want more than one thing from her. That I want more than casual sex with her. That I want the whole package. Her smart mouth and brilliant mind. Her shapely body and sutured heart. All of it. The only way I know to show her this is to deprive myself of the one thing I am synonymous with — sex.

It may not be the perfect answer to show her I care. But it is the only way I know. For now.

And she doesn't seem to mind. Not one bit.

TEN
PEYTON

LAST NIGHT FEELS LIKE A DREAM. A really fucking good dream. One of those dreams you never want to wake from, but inevitably do. The ones you can't revisit, no matter how quickly you fall back asleep.

Being known as a town whore isn't always the best title for anyone—man or woman. But the experience Micah has gained from said relations… let's just say no one will hear me complain. Not once.

The man weaves witchcraft with his tongue. Spins gold with the tip. Just the tip. And could make my shower singing voice Grammy-worthy in just one night. That is pure talent.

My experience with men—as far as number of partners—is minuscule in comparison to Micah. The few relationships I had were long term, the shortest a year and a half. Each man had his own talents or mannerisms I loved —a specific maneuver, the way he touched my cheek, how he looked at me like no one was in the room. Each of them sweet in their own way. Each of them someone I cared for deeply at the time.

But none of them shared similarities with Micah. Which strikes me as odd. Looking back at my past relationships, all the men shared identical physical features and comparable ways of thinking. All of them were the complete opposite of Micah. Part of me wonders if it was my brain's way of sheltering me from the past. Steering me away from men like the one I crushed on, but crushed me in a different way.

Compared to the men of my past, Micah Reed is wild. Untamed. Unrestrained. With the words that leave his lips and the tricks he performs with his tongue.

But Micah has also displayed a tender side; a side he keeps hidden from those not in his inner circle. This is the side of Micah that holds my gaze as if nothing exists but me and him and the moment shared between us. This side remembers my food preferences and what shows I watch and the spot to kiss that makes me melt. The playful side that spurs me on for fun, makes me laugh and puts a smile on my face.

Micah Reed is a true anomaly. A mysterious man with countless layers to unfold. A man who puts on a decent front, but harbors much more within himself. With what happened with his ex, I get not allowing your heart to be vulnerable. But at some point, if he wants more out of life, he will need to expose himself emotionally more than ever. Especially if he wants our relationship to evolve.

"Hellcat!"

I snap my head up from the glass I cleaned for the last however many minutes. Surprised I haven't scrubbed the bar logo off in the process. Glancing down the bar, I spy Micah looking my way with a cocked brow.

Great. I will never hear the end of this.

After I set the glass down, I spin to face him. "Yes?" I draw out the one-worded question.

"Been calling you the last five minutes. Need a break?"

Five minutes? No fucking way have I been washing the same glass, spaced out, for five minutes. I narrow my eyes. He is messing with me, right?

Rather than holler down the bar, especially with every set of female eyes in the club on us, I walk the short distance and aim for a quieter conversation. Well, as quiet as a conversation can be with karaoke playing in the background.

"One," I say when I reach him. "You have *not* been calling my name that long." He opens his mouth to interrupt, but I hold up a hand. He snaps his mouth shut and flashes me a lopsided smile. "Two, what makes you think I need a break? We've only been open an hour."

The other corner of his mouth curves up and presents me with the most wicked grin to don his lips. A grin that trickles a thrill in my veins and dampens my panties. A mischievous smile that hints at secrets only we share and heats my skin from crown to root.

He shrugs, then tilts his head. "You look a little tired. Like you were up past your bedtime."

Smart-ass.

I step closer. His starry eyes playful as his tongue darts out to lick his lips. Taking another step in his direction, I inhale his cologne and refuse to exhale until necessary. The scent dances in my nasal cavities, swirls in my lungs, then takes up residence in my memory. It has me begging for more of him. Another taste of his lips, his tongue. But I won't tell him that. Not here. Not yet.

"I'm a big girl, starlight." I toss a smirk his way. "And I go to bed when I'm ready." My tongue sweeps over my lips and I bite and hold the lower for one, two, three breaths before releasing. Micah shifts his weight from right to left as I lean in, my lips less than an inch from his ear. "Maybe you should've offered me yours."

Micah sucks in a sharp breath, then releases it. Heat paints my skin as his breathing spikes. I startle when fingers tug at the hem of my shirt. Claw at my hip bone. Neither of us takes a step back. The bar may be packed with women wanting fruity cocktails and countless people hoping to make it big on stage, but they all vanish.

Right now, all I hear, all I see, all I feel is Micah.

Memories of last night play on a repetitive loop. The gentle and hungry ways his fingers caressed my skin. How he worshiped me with his lips. And how he took my body to places I never knew existed.

Yes, I have orgasmed with other partners—and myself. But what happened last night… that was not just oral and orgasms. Something else simmered beneath the surface. As if a dormant piece of me woke up and opened her eyes for the first time.

And I can't get enough.

"Best be careful what you ask for, hellcat." He kisses beneath my ear and a shiver rolls up my spine. "I make good on my promises. Do you?"

Before I open my mouth to respond, a female voice grabs both our attention. "Well, don't you two look nonproductive at work."

We simultaneously inch back, but stay within reach. A twin pair of starry eyes stare at us. When I broaden my view, six other sets of eyes leer at us. Their expressions range from *way to go* to *that's interesting*. No matter how they regard me or us, I don't want to be seen like the other women Micah has been with. Easy and replaceable.

Thankfully, none of them look at me in this manner. Perhaps because they never met any of the women Micah bedded. Works in my favor.

"What's up, Shell?"

She rolls her eyes and points to the makeshift stage as if the answer is obvious. "Karaoke, big brother. It may be out of our way, but we're here for it. Plus, we get to see you."

Although I have hung out with everyone opposite us, I remain quiet. Not that I feel uncomfortable in their presence or sparking conversation. My personal relationship with each of them is still new. With new people, I tend to be more reserved and less of an open book. Talkative, but not open.

Cora and Autumn smile, the corners of their eyes lifting with the gesture. Cora nudges Shelly. "Let's grab a table." Then Cora returns her attention to me. "You guys able to sit with us for a song or two? Or does it get super busy?"

I open my mouth to tell her we have other stuff to do, but Micah beats me to the punch.

"Sure." He glances my way. "Give us a few to wrap up paperwork in the office."

Shelly nods at her brother, but I see the *sure you have paperwork to do* glint in her eye. Because in what universe does it take two of us to plug numbers into spreadsheets for an average-sized nightclub/bar? Simple answer—it doesn't.

Do I correct him? Nope. Because after our conversation moments ago, I am dying to have his lips on mine again. Dying to taste and tangle tongues with him.

"Sure thing, big brother."

The group wanders to two vacant tall tops and scoots them closer together. Jake greets them and takes their drink order. Before Jake brings over the order, Micah starts popping off beer lids and mixing drinks. He knows his friends—family—well.

"Why don't you head back to the office," he suggests. "I'll be there in a few."

"Micah…" I start with a laugh. "Do they honestly believe we both need to do paperwork? It takes one of us a couple hours, at most, to get through it."

He stops shaking the drink, sets it down and steps into

my personal space. "They have no clue what our job entails. Even if they did, I wouldn't give a fuck." Another step in my direction and we are toe to toe. Heat radiates off him and is like a match to my libido. "Go. I'll be there soon."

I drop the towel I picked up at some point and start for the office. As I pass the group, I give a courteous wave and smile. Seven return my way. When I reach the hall and step out of sight, my stride kicks into high gear. Once in the office, I shut the door but leave it unlocked.

With no idea when Micah will waltz in or what he had in mind, I plop down in the desk chair and get to work. Whether or not it is his intention for us to actually work, invoices and orders still need to get done.

Thirty minutes later, I input the third invoice and set it in the "to be filed" pile. As I pick up the next, the office door swings open and Micah strides in. He studies me behind the desk, licks his lips, and locks the door.

Dear lord, someone help me with this man.

"Almost done," I croak out as he saunters across the room.

"Good. Means we have more time."

"More—"

Before I finish the question, he spins the chair so I face him, bends down and smashes my lips with his. Stunned, it takes me two swipes of his lips over mine before I react. Then I fist his shirt and haul him closer. The chair slides back, smacks into the wall, and we laugh.

Micah loops his hands under my arms and stands me

up. He brings his lips back to mine, snakes his arms around my waist, and walks us toward the couch. Carefully, he lowers himself to sit on the couch, then hauls me forward so I straddle him.

Fingers grip my hips, my ass as I rock against him. Lips and tongues and teeth assault each other, hungry. Starved. Downright famished. He breaks the kiss and licks his way down the column of my throat. A hand palms my breast, pinches my nipple between the material.

Fire and ache and titillation course through my veins, awaken every nerve ending, and scorch every square inch of my skin. If we were anywhere else, I would rip off my shirt then his. Press our bare flesh together and taste him.

But we aren't somewhere else. And I will *not* take this next level at work. At least that is what I tell myself.

"Micah." His name jagged and breathy on my tongue as I grind against his erection. "We have to…" God, this feels so fucking good. "We need to…" He nips at the skin along my collarbone and my eyes roll back. "Stop," I pant out. "We need to stop."

He licks from the thick strap of my top to the hollow of my throat. I rock against his hips and moan in his ear.

"You want this to stop, hellcat? You're gonna need to stop doing that," he mumbles into the crook of my neck.

Did I say I *wanted* this to stop? The word *want* never left my lips. No. Because I *want* this to continue. More than anything. But we *need* to stop. Not that she has in quite a while, but Ani—or Sean—could waltz into Roar at any moment. Last thing either of us needs is to have just-fucked hair and rumpled clothes.

I inch back and lock eyes with Micah. The starry gold flecks in his dark irises smolder. Burn hot and beg for more as he continues to fist my hips.

"Never said want," I say, my voice gruff and wobbly.

His brows pinch above his nose. "Huh?"

"You said if I *wanted* this to stop… I never said want. Need is what I said. That we need to stop."

He drops his forehead to my shoulder and groans. "Why do you have to be right?" And I love how his whiny and muffled words vibrate my skin, my chest. I comb my fingers through his hair, scrape his scalp with my nails. The pads of his fingers dig into my hips as a groan rumbles up his throat. "Better stop doing that or we won't stop."

Huffing out a breath, I lean away and force myself off his lap. I offer my hand once upright. "Come on, starlight. If you want to hang with your friends, we need to get some actual work done."

Micah takes my hand, rises from the couch and adjusts himself. "I'll finish with the invoices if you'll work on ordering."

"Deal," I tell him.

When we keep our hands to ourselves, work actually gets accomplished. Over the next hour, we wrap up the invoices, file them away, and input a supply order. Everything done and back in its rightful place, we head for the door.

But before I unlock it, Micah whips me around and pins me to the door. He clutches my chin between his thumb and forefinger. Eyes locked on mine. Lips a breath away.

"Kiss me. Before we leave this room and have to force ourselves to maintain a distance, kiss me."

This side of Micah is so new. His urgency to have me. To taste me. Feel me. Possess me. It calls out to my baser instincts. Wakes me up and revitalizes parts I didn't know were asleep.

As for his steady demand for me to kiss him…

With his grip still on my chin, I lean closer. But rather than give him the kiss he craves, I lick up the stubble on his chin, over his lips and stop at the top of his philtrum. He reacts with unfathomable speed.

Micah wraps his fingers around my wrists and pins them over my head. Presses his hips to mine and locks me in place—not that I planned on moving. Slides a foot between mine and kicks my feet out. Then leans in and traces the tip of his nose up the column of my throat, stopping just below my ear.

"Tsk, tsk, hellcat. Really should be mindful of your actions. You wanted me on my best behavior, but that… you just handed over your one-way ticket. There's no going back."

My chest heaves, nipples taut and chafing the material of my bra and shirt. With the taste of him on my tongue, his scent invading my nose, his body pressed to mine…

fuck, I am tempted to provoke the beast. Within him and me.

"One-way ticket?" I wheeze out.

He gyrates his hips, his erection unyielding as it rubs my clit through my pants and his.

"Mmhm." A hand trails down my arm, the side of my torso and lands on my hip. His tongue darts out and licks the spot beneath my ear. And I don't fight the shiver that rolls through my body. "Best hold on, hellcat."

Before I ask what he means, he drops to his knees in front of me. Deft fingers make quick work of the button and zipper on my pants. Two breaths later, my pants are at my ankles as he traces his nose along the fabric of my panties. Inhaling deeply, his palms slide up my thighs, grasp the thin straps of my underwear and wiggle them down, down, down.

We shouldn't be doing this. Not at work.

Then his tongue drags leisurely over my lower lips and I forget everything. The office, the fact half my clothes are missing, the club and people outside this room. All of it… gone.

Micah shimmies a foot out of my clothes, spreads my legs wider, hikes one over his shoulder and devours me like his last meal. One of my hands fists his hair while the other clutches the door handle. I grind myself on his mouth, moan as he slips a finger inside me, then another, and revel in the abrasiveness of his stubble against my sensitive skin.

The back of my head smacks the door as I tug his hair.

Grind harder. Faster. Unladylike moans crawl up my throat and spill from my lips. His fingers pick up speed as he sucks my clit between his lips. My legs tremble and breaths come in short bursts. I slam my eyes shut as the room spins.

Then Micah performs sorcery in a one-two combo with his tongue and fingers. Stars light the back of my lids. Shock waves surge through my body as the orgasm pulses over and over. My legs give out and he grabs my hips to keep me upright.

Again and again, he licks up my seam. Feasts on every drop of my orgasm as I quiver atop him. Slowly rises to his feet then slams his mouth down on mine.

The taste of me on his tongue does libidinous things to my body. I fist his shirt and drag our bodies flush. Suck his tongue like I plan to his dick when given the opportunity.

"You taste like fucking nirvana and sin," he groans against my lips.

"Wait until you experience it too."

"Fuck," he whisper-hisses. "How the hell can I leave the room now?"

I laugh, haul his lips back to mine, and kiss him with unrestrained aggression. As his hands glide from my hip up my abdomen, I break the kiss and shove him back a step.

"We should stop." I say the words, but they hold no umph. Because right now, all I want to do is shed his clothes and drop to my knees. Worship him in ways I never have, in ways he has never known.

Who knew Micah Reed would turn me into a craved vixen? Certainly not me. But here we are.

He palms his cock as I reach for my panties and slip them back on, followed by my pants. Zipper up and button in place, I walk over to the small mirror in the office and work to make my hair resemble what it did prior to Micah entering the office. In the end, I twist it in a topknot and say fuck it.

After I swipe a fresh coat of gloss on my lips, I spin to face Micah. "You know we can't walk out of here at the same time."

He lifts a brow as the corner of his mouth kicks up. "Why?"

"One—I look freshly fucked." This garners a bigger smile from him. "Two—it would just be odd. We're never both in here together this long in the first place. To walk out of here at the same time would definitely bring unwanted attention our way."

"Who says it's unwanted?"

"Me," I say on a sigh. "Micah, the last thing we need is the staff thinking we're acting inappropriately. And that they can do the same." I shake my head before dropping my gaze to the floor. "I've worked hard to get here. If anyone even remotely believes I slept with my boss to get promoted…"

"Hey." Micah steps up to me, pinches my chin between his thumb and forefinger, and lifts until our eyes lock. "That is not what's happening here." The edge to his words sharp enough to sever any doubt.

"You and I know that." I point toward the main part of the club. "They don't, though." My eyes glaze over. "Please, can we just go back out there? You first and I'll follow in a few."

"Under one condition." He steps closer and we stand toe to toe.

"What?"

"I don't want to hide this. Us." He trails a single fingertip from the hollow of my throat to the v of my shirt. "Working here isn't the same as a corporate job. Rules are different. More flexible. Besides, I think Ani knows about us and she doesn't seem bothered by it."

Considering Ani and I have been friends for years, she definitely knows more about Micah than he realizes. Nothing outlandish. I do keep some things private. But I shared our history with her. And where our relationship resides now—minus the intimate details. Gossip over such personal aspects of my life will never happen. No matter how close I am with someone. In my opinion, certain things should stay between the two people involved.

"She knows."

He shifts to hold my gaze easier. "Yeah? And she's cool with us?"

My entire frame sags. "Yes," I mumble.

"What's that?"

"You're such a pain in the ass." I straighten my spine

and roll my eyes. "Yes, she knows about us. Kind of. Not the nitty-gritty, but that we've been hanging out."

"And?" My brows inch up as I look away. "She's fine with it, isn't she?"

Micah Reed lives to drive me insane. I just know it. Of course, Ani is fine with Micah and me being together. As long as our relationship doesn't interfere with work or cause future problems, Ani has no issue with us being together. In any capacity.

"Mmhm." I nod.

"Then why are you so worked up?"

He doesn't get it. Either that or he doesn't comprehend how other people may perceive the situation. Anyone with eyes would have seen me and Micah close prior to the official promotion. It wouldn't matter that the job had been offered to me months back. Some people may still assume I slept my way up the ladder.

And that... is not acceptable.

"Have you ever been a woman?" I ask the question knowing I will get a smart-ass answer. But I hold up a hand before he gets a word out. "No, you haven't. So, you don't understand what it's like. To have to bust your ass ten times harder for the same opportunity. To work extra just to show you're worthy of the same pay. It isn't our fault we were born with different parts between our legs and on our chest, but our part of the world was founded by men. And most of society doesn't see men and women as equals." I close my eyes, take a deep breath, and reopen them. "So, please... do this for me.

Straighten your clothes and hair, walk out of here, and pretend like we were working back here and nothing else."

Warm hands engulf mine as Micah erases any remaining space between us. He lifts my hands and deposits them on his shoulders, then snakes his around my waist.

"Sorry," he whispers, inches from my lips. "I have no intention of flaunting what you and I do behind closed doors. But Peyton?" I meet his starry night eyes. "I won't hide our relationship. Not saying I plan to walk up to everyone and tell them. But this…" He presses his lips to mine briefly. "You aren't some dirty secret or sidepiece. For you, I'll walk out of here alone. But make no mistake, if someone asks about our relationship status, I won't lie. We haven't defined us, but there is an us."

He kisses me once more, steps back and walks out the door. No tension or awkwardness lingers. Just Micah giving me the space I need while fulfilling my request. When the door shuts after him, I take a deep breath and collect myself—physically and mentally. Organize my thoughts on what happened over the last thirty minutes and stash them for later conversation, when we are alone.

I take one last glance in the mirror, brush my hands down my outfit, and head for the door. Each step away from the office weighs heavily. But the moment I hit the main club floor, spot Shelly and Cora on the karaoke stage making asses of themselves to Wreckx-N-Effect's "Rump Shaker," I breathe easier.

No eyes dart my direction. No whispers or pointed fingers. Everything is just... normal.

After checking in with the staff, I join Micah at the table with Gavin, Trevor, Erin, Jonas, and Autumn. Cora and Shelly still dominate the karaoke machine while the crowd cheers them on. For a moment, I sit beside Micah and enjoy myself. Enjoy the laughter of the people nearby. Enjoy the ease at being with this group of people and with Micah.

Cora and Shelly skip off the stage when the song ends, park on their stools, and sip their drinks. A fifty-something woman picks up the mic and preps for her song to start. When the intro of the song spills from the club speakers, everyone at the table goes wide eyed. Cora and Shelly set their drinks down and spin to face the woman on stage who breathes heavily into the mic with the intro of "My Humps" by Black Eyed Peas.

"Thought Karaoke Nights at our hangout were great, but this..." Cora points to the stage. "This is gold."

Micah leans in and kisses my temple. "You good?"

My eyes do another scan of the club, the staff, the group at the table. No one bats an eyelash my way. No one curls their lip or rolls an eye. Life continues to exist around us as if this is normal. As if *we* are normal. And I have never loved the feeling more.

"Yeah."

"Peyton!" My gaze darts to Shelly, who all but bounces on her stool. "Hang out with us on Sunday."

I scan the two tables, take in the other sets of eyes

peering my way. Cora leans into Gavin as they both give me a content smile. Jonas wraps his arm around Autumn's shoulders before they both nod. Trevor and Erin smile my way before she rejoins a conversation with Cora and he looks back at his phone.

How many years did I want this form of acceptance? To have my own people. Yes, I have Reese and love everything he brings to my life. But I always felt like something was missing. I always wanted more. Like dreaming of the big family you never had but wished you did.

Is that what this is? An opportunity at my own family. Maybe.

"I'll be there."

Beneath the table, Micah rests a hand on my thigh and squeezes. Our eyes lock and something new passes between us. An unnamed emotion. A flicker. The start of something more.

The start of us.

ELEVEN

MICAH

I peer over my shoulder at Shelly and laugh. Did she really leave that comment wide open? My sweet baby sister. Naive and not in the same breath.

"That's what she said."

Shelly slaps my bicep. "Shut up, asshole. Seriously, though. Who's going to eat it all?" She points to the grill where Jonas flips burgers, brats, chicken, and ribs.

It is a lot of food, but Sunday always involves this much or close to it. Our Sunday get-togethers have slowly evolved into a massive gathering and tend to last several hours. The food gets eaten. If not, Autumn packs it up and ships it out with us as we leave. Which is a win for me since my kitchen skills still suck.

"Considering close to twenty people will be here, it won't go to waste. Why're you freaking out? You're never this antsy."

Shelly isn't the quietest person among us, but also not the most exuberant. That award goes to Penny. But I know my sister. Her fretting over the amount of food is… weird. Then again, she has her moments. I find it best not to question the change unless instinct tells me otherwise.

Her hands plop down on her hips. "I'm *not* freaking out." Then she storms into the house where Cora and Autumn work on side dishes.

"Dude, what's up with your sister?" Gavin asks as he grabs a beer from the cooler.

Sipping from my own bottle, I shrug. "Who knows. Probably something or someone irritating her and I'm her scapegoat today." If she continues with the theatrics, I will pull her aside later and ask more probing questions.

Gavin, Jonas, and I shoot the shit while the ladies are inside. Still early, only the six of us here, we catch up on monotonous stuff. Work, homelife, day to day boring stuff.

Gavin tells us about an upcoming photo shoot for sportswear. No travel is involved, which makes him and Cora both happy. Before coming back to Florida, Gavin traveled extensively for work. But once he and Cora reunited, they don't leave each other's side often. Can't say I blame them after spending so much time apart.

Jonas says his dad continues to hint at working less. His dad working less at the garage equals him slowly taking over the business. He always knew the day would come, but the fact it is happening has him slightly on edge.

I share how busy work has been since the changes

made in early June. It sucks not seeing Peyton at work four nights a week, but we would never get things done if we worked every shift together. But with each passing week, we spend more and more time together outside of work. And I want more.

As if my thoughts summon her, Peyton walks out the back door and down the steps. Arm hooked with Shelly's, they laugh at something I wasn't privy to hear. No doubt, Shelly told her an embarrassing story of my younger days. I expect nothing less.

"Hey," I say as she approaches and unhooks from Shelly. "Glad you made it." I kiss her temple and wrap an arm around her waist. "Drink?"

"Please. And did you think I wouldn't show?" she asks with a chuckle.

With reluctance, I drop my hand from her waist, set my beer down, fetch one from the cooler for her, pop the top and hand it over. "I never want to assume anything when it comes to you." I guide us over to the loungers and sit. "How was Gulfside?"

Her face falls as her frame caves. "Good. I miss being there as often."

Peyton went from working two weekday shifts at the assisted living facility to one. Then, two weeks ago, she cut it back to every other Sunday. Roar doesn't interfere with her days at the facility, but the extra hours at the club and spending time with me have stretched her thin.

Wrapping an arm around her, I stroke up and down her spine. "Sure they miss you too."

Before either of us get another word out, cacophony erupts as Penny, Rex, Reznor, Tatyana, and Ashton walk outside. Clementine steals Ashton from his mom and they run into the yard with Spartan hot on their heels and laughter in the air. Greetings and hugs are exchanged before new conversations start.

Three rock ballads later, everyone has a plate in their hands and is piling it high with a little of everything. I tease Peyton at the excessive amount of food on her plate, even though I don't give a fuck. I simply love our banter. She tosses me the middle finger, then shoves a coleslaw-covered brat between her lips.

Fuck me.

I groan and bunch the cotton of my shirt near my zipper in an effort to disguise my stiffening cock. Sensing my hopefully not obvious discomfort, Peyton brings her lips to my ear. "Need help?"

Of all the things I expected her to say, that was not one of them. A tease, yes. Offering assistance with my *dilemma*, no. I choke on the heaping forkful of potato salad I shoveled in my mouth seconds ago.

Peyton sets her plate and mine on the table, lifts my hands over my head, then slaps my back. My face turns red—not only from inhaling food but also embarrassment —as tears spill down my cheeks. The cough doesn't quit and almost has me laughing.

Rising from the lounger, Peyton takes my hand and hauls me inside. "Be right back," she tells everyone as we head for the house.

Inside, she steers us into the bathroom, shuts the door and locks it.

"What are you…" My cough, lighter this time, cuts me off. Before I finish the question, Peyton reaches forward and grabs me. More specifically, my cock.

"Offering to help." She bats her lashes and strokes me through my shorts.

I grind against her and growl. "No chance in hell I'm letting you get me off in this tiny-ass bathroom."

Her grip tightens. "Why not?" she asks, breath hot on my neck.

"The first time I get off with you will be after hours of foreplay." *Holy hell.* If she doesn't stop, my shorts will flaunt evidence of our bathroom escapade in no time.

"Foreplay, huh?" she purrs in my ear and my eyes roll back.

I grip her hand and stop her teasing. "Yes." Unwillingly, my fingers peel hers away. "Lucky for you, we have hours ahead of us."

She lifts a brow. "You speak as if *tonight*, here, is foreplay."

I bring her hand to my lips and kiss each knuckle in turn. "She gets it," I whisper. "Hope you're ready, hellcat."

Dropping her hand, I adjust myself then waltz out of the bathroom with an ear-to-ear smile. Not until I reach the door do I hear Peyton rushing to follow me out.

When we return to our seats on the patio, half the group looks our way. We weren't gone long, but definitely longer than necessary. I don't give a fuck, let them think of all the possible things we didn't do that we could have.

After no one says a word for too long, I tap my throat. "Potato got stuck." I shrug, pick up my plate, and act as if nothing happened.

Peyton, on the other hand, has rosy cheeks. *Way to put our bathroom rendezvous on display.* I love it.

The next ten minutes pass uneventful. Beer, food, music and good conversation occupy the group. Peyton turns her attention to Penny and Autumn as they talk about weird tattoo placement. Penny recants the story of some guy who had the word *sweet* tattooed on his right ass cheek.

As Peyton goes to respond, I set my hand on her thigh and slowly trail it toward her midline. She sucks in a breath and doesn't say a word. Penny drones on about Mr. Sweet Cheek, not realizing I cut Peyton off.

Peyton doesn't move. Doesn't shift her attention. She keeps her eyes forward and pretends to listen, nodding at the appropriate times.

Inch by inch, my fingers dance over her skin. Slide over the exposed flesh and toy with the frayed hemline of her denim shorts. The action hidden from observation by the empty plate in her hands. The tip of my pinkie slips under the denim and she shifts her weight. The outside of her thigh presses firmly against mine as her thighs part imperceptibly to anyone looking. But I feel the change. Her breath hitches and skin pinks.

Much as I love the reaction, I remove my hand and bring my lips to her ear. "Dessert?"

She huffs out a laugh. "Yes." The huskiness in her voice pauses my rise from the lounger. I take my plate and hers, deposit them in the bin, and load up a single plate with sweets.

Most of the night at Jonas and Autumn's continues much the same. Me toying with Peyton while she tries to carry on as if I don't affect her. A brush of the arm. Graze of the thigh. Breath near her neck. Hand on her lower back. With each touch, I pick up on her twitches and startled moves. Subtle enough no one speaks up. Obvious enough, I detect every single one.

Then I switch gears. Drape an arm over her shoulders and draw circles on her skin with my fingertips. Drop my lips every few minutes to her hair, her temple, the angle of her jaw and leave chaste kisses. Toy with the ends of her hair or the hemline of her top.

Reznor announces their departure. While hugs get exchanged, I lean closer and whisper in Peyton's ear. "Want to go?" My thumb strokes her shoulder. "To my place."

Twisting enough to face me, Peyton's eyes dart between mine. Two dazzling violet irises glitter in the dim light of the tiki torches. The way she regards me, the way she searches for answers to questions left unspoken, brings doubt to the surface. With Peyton, I never want to presume. She may have forgiven me for past discretions, but that doesn't mean she has forgotten.

Her tongue darts out and licks her lips, slow and calculated. The corner of her mouth kicks up when my eyes drop and follow the action. After a beat, I bring my eyes back to hers. Study the intent behind her stare since she has yet to answer.

Reznor and Tatyana step up to the lounger, ready to bid us good night. But I want Peyton's answer before they do.

"Promise to behave," I whisper, hoping it will provoke a response.

At this, she cocks a brow. "What if I don't want you to?"

Hello, hellcat.

"Then maybe I won't." I nudge my head toward the door. "Shall we."

She tips her head left and right as if pondering the idea. As Reznor all but begs for a goodbye hug, she answers, "Yes."

One word is all it takes and my mind goes through all the steps we need to take to leave like civilized people. We rise from the lounger, say good night to Reznor and Tatyana. Then we go through the process with everyone else. I do my best to act casual. Behave as if there is no rush. When, in fact, my feet won't move fast enough and the hugs seem to never end.

Finally, we escape out the front door and I walk Peyton to her car. "See you in a few." She nods.

I hop into my truck and crank the engine. As I throw the truck in reverse, I coach myself to not speed on the way home. Traffic violations will only add misery to the evening. But damn, am I eager to have Peyton all to myself. Eager to see how this night ends. Because once she is in my bed, there is no going back.

TWELVE
PEYTON

A FEW BLOCKS from Micah's house, I text Reese while at a stoplight.

Peyton: Might not be home tonight. FYI
Reese: I expect details.

I don't respond. Last thing I need is an endless back-and-forth exchange with Reese before possibly taking my relationship with Micah next level. Reese is the brother I never had. And who talks with their brother before making out—or more—with someone. Certainly not me.

Micah parks in the driveway and I pull in behind him. Turning off the headlights, I cut the engine, stare out the windshield, and take a deep breath.

"This is Micah," I mumble to myself as I watch him exit his truck. "The man you've been kissing for weeks. The man who's gone down on you." He steps closer to my car and I take another deep breath. "Don't go acting shy now."

One last deep inhale through my nose, then I open the door on the exhale. I lock the car before he takes my hand and guides us inside. Neither of us says a word, but the silence is pleasant. Tranquil and a little energizing.

With each button he presses to unlock the door, my pulse thumps a faster rhythm. A thin layer of moisture slicks my palms and I pray to whoever hears my call to not let Micah notice.

As we step into the house, I expect him to maul me. To slam me against the door and crush my mouth with his. Pin my hands over my head and grind his erection against the junction of my thighs. Moan my name and bite my lip.

But none of this happens.

We step inside and he guides us to the couch. Gives me a chaste kiss on the lips, lets go of my hand and goes to the fridge for water. After a sip, he offers me one. I take it in the hopes it will cool off my immeasurable fever and wake my rational side.

Does he sense my low-level anxiety over what might happen? God, how embarrassing. I feel like a trembling virgin. Who knows why? My virginity flew out the window more than a decade ago. And I haven't exactly been celibate—although, it has been a while.

When he turns the television on and starts an episode of *Supernatural*, I start to second-guess every thought from tonight. We kick off our shoes and settle into the couch. When he tugs me closer to him, I stop thinking and sag into the warmth of his frame. After fifteen minutes, my anxiety vanishes and I curl into his side and rest my head on his shoulder.

Three-quarters through the episode, Micah kisses the top of my head. The gesture sweet as his lips linger for a beat. I tip my chin up to return the kiss. The act natural and innocent.

Until the kiss evolves. Grows from chaste pecks to the delicacy of tasting lips. Slow and gentle mixed with heat and the occasional scrape of his stubble.

A hand cups my cheek. Fingers weave through the hair at the base of my skull as he draws me closer and keeps me in place. A match strikes beneath my breastbone when his tongue traces the seam of my lips. The chambers of my heart pound, pound, pound against my rib cage as I gasp and his tongue slips in and tangles with mine.

And then everything explodes. Detonates like a ticking time bomb.

I fist his shirt, throw a leg over his lap, and straddle him. Rock my hips and rub against the thick bulge beneath his zipper. Tangle his tongue with mine before I suck it like a popsicle.

He clamps down on my hips hard enough to bruise me for days. Adds more pressure where I stroke him through our clothes. Sits up straighter, trails a hand up my spine until he reaches the base of my skull, wraps my hair around his fist and jerks my head back.

The motion stings my scalp as I gasp for air. He sucks and bites his way down the column of my throat. Kneads my hip with his other hand. Paints his tongue along my collarbone. My hands glide up his chest, snake around his neck, take hold of his hair and yank. Hard.

His lips break from my skin in a hiss. *"Fuck."*

Before I voice a comeback, he scoops under my ass and stands. His lips back on mine as we move through the house. Greed and hunger taste so fucking sweet on his tongue.

And then I am airborne. But not long.

In the dark room, I land on a cloud. Micah crawls up the bed and reinstates our kiss. His hands at the bottom hem of my shirt inch up my body—slow, too slow—as they tug the material away. Lips and teeth and tongue imprint my skin as he unclasps my bra. The skimpy fabric gets tossed aside and replaced with his mouth.

I thread my fingers through his hair as I arch my back and press my breasts into his hungry mouth. He grips my wrists, breaks my hold on him, and pins my hands to the mattress. Clamps down on my nipple before popping it from his lips and paying equal attention to the other.

"Micah," I whisper-moan into the darkness.

He releases my nipple and hovers above me. Stars burn white hot in his dark irises as he holds my gaze. The intensity in his irises slicks my skin, and I swallow.

"Keep your hands here," he commands in a thick baritone. I nod and he shakes his head. "No, Peyton. In here, you need to use words."

"Yes," I whisper. "Won't move my hands."

"That's my hellcat."

He drops his lips back to mine, kisses me one, two, three times before sucking my lower lip between his. Then his lips leave mine and kiss a trail of fire up the line of my jaw. Nibble on my earlobe as my eyes roll back. Suck the tender skin beneath my ear as I grind my clit against his erection.

As his lips move down my neck, he releases my wrists. Skims the tips of his fingers along my forearms, my triceps as he kisses his way down. Fever flares over my body as he tattoos my skin with his tongue. Marks me as his with his teeth. Bruises my flesh with his mouth.

His hands squeeze my breasts, graze the sides of my abdomen, then land on the button of my shorts.

And then he freezes.

I lift my head and glance down my midline. I lock eyes with him as he watches me, studies me, questions me. As he silently asks for permission. As he waits for consent.

"Micah?"

"Yes, hellcat," he purrs, his breath hot on my skin.

"Take my clothes off."

He cocks a brow and tilts his head. "Anything else?"

I love and loathe how he wants me to say the words aloud. I am not a shy lover, but Micah and I haven't traveled this road yet. And I get his need to hear me verbalize what I want.

Sitting up—which causes him to do the same—I come face-to-face with him. Inches separate our lips. My bare breasts a breath from brushing his cotton shirt. I hold his gaze. Read the carnality in his eyes. It adds fuel to the roaring fire beneath my skin. Possesses me. Makes me ravenous.

Without moving my hands, I lean forward, bite his lower lip then growl as I release it. A breath between us, I whisper-hiss, "Fuck me."

Unexpectedly, his eyes widen a beat. A growl rips from his chest and spills from his lips. Then his hand wraps around my throat and constricts as he shoves me back to the mattress. My oxygen is cut off enough to make me dizzy, but not knock me out and I roll my eyes before closing them.

The button on my shorts pops open seconds before he bites the fabric and separates the zipper teeth. Cool air stings my lungs when he removes his hand from my throat. The mattress shifts before his hands scoop my ass cheeks and he shimmies my shorts and panties down my thighs.

Completely bare on his comforter, he stands at the foot of the bed, palms his cock, and licks his lower lip. My hands itch to reach down, not to cover myself, but to touch myself too. But I resist the urge and let him visually devour me.

Micah traces his fingers up my shins, then slides them back down to my ankles, takes hold and yanks my ass to the edge of the bed before dropping to his knees. He hooks my left leg over his shoulder, followed by my right. Lips press to the inside of my thigh. Teeth nip their way up, up, up my thigh, tongue tasting me along the way.

When he reaches the apex of my thighs, he licks everywhere but where I want him. Teases me with slight touches. Tortures me with occasional bites. Makes me moan as he marks my flesh on the upper part of my inner thigh.

Then he licks my lips, bottom to clit, and hums his appreciation. "Fuck, I love how sweet you taste." Before rational thought forms from his words, his mouth is on me. Lapping and sucking, tasting and devouring. He adds a finger, rubs that sweet spot inside me. Flicks his tongue over my clit again and again before inserting a second finger.

I fist the comforter as my back bows off the mattress. Thighs clamp the angle of his jaw. Ankles hook behind his head and force him into me as I rock against his mouth. Against the scrape of his stubble. Against the perfect strokes of his tongue and drive of his fingers.

Heat builds between my legs, curls up my spine, blooms across my chest, up my neck, over my cheeks. Consumes me in every possible way as Micah picks up speed. Curls his digits and pumps faster. Sucks my clit between his lips and performs voodoo on my body.

In the past, I had never been a vocal lover. Never moaned or screamed or cried out a name in pleasure. But with Micah, I whimper. Mewl for more. Beg him not to stop. Moan his name like it pains me not to.

He makes me wanton. Carnal. Hungry for only him.

And the way he looks at me now—eager to consume every part of me—sets me off. Has me fisting the comforter and cursing at the ceiling. Tremors rock me head to toe. Blind me in the darkness. Steal my breath and stall my heart.

"So fucking sweet," he says on a moan as he licks the orgasm from my skin.

As the shaking settles, I shift to my hands and knees. Crawl to where he stands at the foot of the bed, shorts tented by his erection. He grins down at me lasciviously.

"Whatcha going to do, hellcat?" He cups my cheek and tips my chin up so we are eye to eye.

I lick my lips, rock back on my haunches, and reach out to drag him closer. Still fully dressed, I slip my hands under his shirt, force it up and off him. Before the cotton hits the floor, my fingers unbutton his shorts, then slide down the zipper. A low thump sounds in the room as his shorts drop to the floor.

Eyes locked on his, I lean forward and drag my tongue from his navel to his nipple. "Taking what's mine," I state.

"Fuck," he whisper-hisses. He fists my throat, locks me in place, and crashes his lips to mine.

But it is my turn.

I slide a hand up his abdomen, over his pec, and land on his throat. When my fingers tighten, as my nails bite his skin, he releases my neck. Moans in my mouth.

I crawl backward on the mattress and he follows. He plants his knees on the mattress and I shift our positions. Drop my hand to his chest, shove him down and straddle him. Grinding myself against him and soak his boxer briefs.

His eyes roll back briefly as he grips my hips. "Confession."

I wiggle my way down his body and reach for the band of his boxer briefs. "This isn't church, Micah. But feel free to worship me."

I yank his briefs down and off, then toss them aside. I rake my gaze over him and stop when I reach his cock. *Sweet fucking Jesus.* The size makes me stutter mentally, but that isn't what has me praying for mercy. No, what makes me swallow and crawl closer are the three barbells.

When my eyes flash to his, a smirk kicks up the corner of his mouth. He tucks an arm under his head and fists his cock with the free hand. "As I started to say—"

"You're building a ladder," I interrupt and tilt my head. "Lucky for you, I'm into construction."

As he opens his mouth with what I bet is a witty comment, I bend down and lick the length of him.

"Dear god," he hisses out as he fists the comforter. A hand comes to the back of my neck and tightens as he hauls me up his body.

"Wasn't done," I mumble against his lips.

He flips me over. "Don't care." With a rock of his hips, he rubs the piercings over my clit. My eyes roll back as I dig my nails into his obliques. "Fuck." Another hiss from his lips. "I need to be inside you."

"What's taking so long then?" I lick along his jawline, then bite the angle of his jaw.

Fingers comb through my hair, fist the locks and yank

to the side. He nips and peppers kisses over my cheek, my jaw, my throat until he reaches my ear.

"I need to *feel* you, Peyton." He lifts enough for our gazes to meet. "I'm clean. Got tested weeks ago. Haven't been with anyone in months."

"I'm on the pill."

Although more than a year passed since my last boyfriend, I continued birth control. The other benefits were a perk, but I also continued taking them in case someone else came along. Figured no harm, no foul.

In this instance, my indifference paid off.

"Thank fuck."

My hair still in his grip, Micah rocks his hips again and teases my lips and clit with the barbells. I carve new crescent moons into his flesh and bite down at the curve of his neck.

Holy Christ. He hasn't put it in yet and I am ready to claw my name on his back. "Micah." His name a moan on my lips.

"Patience, hellcat." He lowers his lips to mine. "I want to take my time with you. Savor you. Own you."

Dear baby Jesus. Not sure what I did to deserve this delicious torture, but thank you.

Micah continues to take his time. He worships every inch of my body. Focuses on places I never knew I wanted a lover to pay attention to. Places that spark cosmic pleasure. After my body convulses a second time, he finally shows me what sex with ladders is all about.

Needless to say, I will never look at a ladder and not

blush. Micah may have slutted around town more than a year, but I reap the benefits in the end. Because no chance in hell anyone else in the future will enjoy the Micah Reed adventure. Not on my watch. Not after I felt him bare and engraved my name in his flesh with my nails.

It's quite possible I had an out-of-body experience when my third orgasm hit. Or I blacked out. To be honest, the likelihood of both happening is conceivable. I won't discount the chances.

What I do know with certainty… Micah more or less just staked his claim. Marked me as his. Not only on my flesh, but also on my soul.

Micah Reed has no idea what it means to be mine. But from this moment forward, I plan to show him.

THIRTEEN

MICAH

How LONG CAN I get away with watching her like this? With thin lines of sunlight highlighting her hair and skin. With soft blonde lashes fanned out just above her cheekbones. And champagne wavy locks spilled over my pillow.

I don't dare move or breathe too heavily. Don't reach out to brush to wayward strands out of her face and tuck them behind her ear. Don't trace my fingertips over her skin and write secret messages only I can decipher.

That would disturb this moment. And this is solely mine.

Instead, I bask in the sight of her. Her fair skin and peaceful expression as she sleeps. The soft snores from her lips as she dreams, hopefully, of me or us. Relish the memories from last night. Every line and curve of her body under my hands. How she reacted to my touch—the bow of her back, quiver of her muscles, moan of my name.

How we exhausted ourselves, yet it was nowhere near enough.

In the early morning hours, we collapsed in a pile of loose limbs and sated souls.

For more than a year, I have yearned for Peyton. Watched her from the sidelines while I took my frustrations out on nameless and faceless women. Taunted her so I had her attention. Because every second she paid me attention, she gave it to no one else. Even if the attention was negative, I wanted it all to myself. Her irritation and poutiness was, is, such a turn-on. In the beginning, I craved something strictly carnal with Peyton. To blow off steam and get her out of my system. Fulfill a need clawing at my insides.

But now... my need for her is so much more. An unquenched hunger. A deep, primal demand. A vital component of my existence. She floods my veins and occupies my marrow. Spins an endless web beneath my sternum that encases my heart and refuses to relinquish its hold.

It steals my breath and awards me life simultaneously.

My fingers twitch beneath the sheet. Itch to feel the warmth of her skin again. But softer this time. Delicately trace the arch of her brow, the bridge of her nose, the swell of her lips. Twirl her soft hair around my finger and toy with the strands in the sunlight. Kiss her until her our lips or tongues tire, whichever happens first.

Her nose twitches, followed by her lips. A gentle pinch of her lashes as she slowly stirs awake. I train my eyes on every tweak her face and body make as she leaves the land of dreams.

Damn, she's gorgeous.

Lucky doesn't begin to describe how I feel as her violet eyes flutter open and lock with my blues. Countless breaths pass and neither of us says a word. She tucks a hand beneath her cheek as a soft smile brightens her face. Waking up with Peyton in my bed, her angelic features the first thing I see in the morning, is the best way to start the day.

"Morning," I whisper and reach for the fallen hairs on her cheek. Her eyes close at my touch. When they reopen, gray flecks dance against the violet backdrop and render me breathless.

"Good morning." Her voice raspy and soft and sexy as hell. Another trait to add to the long list of characteristics I like about her.

Morning breath be damned, I want to kiss her. Feel her beneath and above me in the early morning hour. Well, early for us.

I quit resisting my need for her and eliminate the space between us. Press my lips to hers, light and tender. Skim a hand down the side of her breast, her waist and stop when I reach her hip. The subdued kiss turns hungry as she throws her leg over my hip. Rocks herself against my cock as her fingers comb my hair and fists the locks.

Within seconds, she has me on my back and straddles my waist. Long champagne locks curtain us as the kiss turns ravenous and she coats my erection with her arousal. On the next circuit up, she shifts so the tip of my cock presses between her lips.

Up and down and up and down. She teases the head of my cock over and over. As I open my mouth to tell her to quit being a tease, she pushes back and fills herself to the hilt.

"Dear god, woman." I fist her hips and keep her in place. "You give religion new meaning."

She sits up, tosses the hair from her face and plants her palms on my chest. "Won't stop you from worshiping me," she says with a rock of her hips. Her hooded eyes look down and pull me into her orbit. "Welcome to heaven."

Peyton rides me like the goddess she is. Head thrown back, tits pushed out, lips parted as her whimpers mingle with the slapping of our bodies. Nails bite my skin to mark me as hers. Marks I will gladly own and flaunt whenever possible.

When her moans and whimpers escalate in pitch, I tighten a hand on her hip and wrap the other around her throat. Piston harder into her sweet, tight pussy. Groan when her walls tighten around me and her claws dig deeper. Revel in the blotchy flush that decorates her breasts, her neck, her cheeks.

And the moment she can no longer hold herself upright, I flip her on her back, hook her legs over my shoulders and drive into her. Skin slapping and grunts echo off the walls as I grip her shoulders and pound her pussy. The violet of her eyes a thin rim around her glassy dilated gaze.

A hand claws its way up my chest and wraps around my throat. Her grip slight as she tugs me down to her lips. Kisses me until her body climbs, climbs, climbs back toward that delicious peak and she gasps for breath.

My pace kicks into fifth gear as I all but slam her body into the headboard. Slide one hand from her shoulder to her throat as I beat her clit with my pelvic bone.

Slap. Slap. Slap.

Her pussy slowly tightens around my cock. Sweet, stuttered cries of pleasure spill from her lips. Nails dig so deep, I swear she pierces my flesh. And it all just adds to the intensity of the moment. Wakes the beast inside me.

Tingling manifests in my balls. Liquid fire slithers up my spine, then winds its way back down. Converges low in my abdomen. Immense pressure and the need to come makes me dizzy, breathless, a slave to the act.

But I hold off. Wait until Peyton gets there first. Wait until her body convulses and milks me.

Hand still on her throat, I lean down and lick her chin, her lips, her cheek. "Let go, hellcat."

I crush my lips to hers. Slam my hips forward and adjust my angle to hit her sweet spot better. Annihilate her clit with my pelvis. Her nails dig deeper. Our bodies slick and hot and on the brink.

Then her walls fist my cock with ferocity. A lyrical staccato of moans echoes in my ears as she trembles beneath me. My next thrust forward ends in a detonation of euphoria as my balls draw up and I release inside Peyton.

For a split second, I feel invincible. On top of the world. Atop the tallest mountain peak, howling at the moon. An incomparable high. A high that dissipates much quicker than Peyton's; her eyes rolled and back arched as her body continues to grind and writhe.

When both our bodies settle, I lower her legs and massage her hips. Then I kiss the fuck out of her. Aggressive at first, then almost submissive and more emotional. She tangles her legs with mine. Wraps me in a full-body embrace. Lightly runs her nails up my back and into my hair.

This single moment more intimate than any other. And it is in this exact moment a warmth builds beneath my sternum. Expands and contracts, conforms and comforts. Takes me prisoner and sets me free.

Much as I want to keep her in my bed all day and night, I can't. Much as I want to kiss her for hours and never release her, I can't. Although early, she needs to start her day before work. And I have to learn how to not be selfish and hoard her from the world.

"C'mon." I break the kiss, slowly sit back on my haunches and offer my hand. "Let's shower. Then I'll make you breakfast."

Peyton takes my hand, scoots off the bed, and holds on to me as her noodle legs give out on the way to the bathroom. She walks all wobbly like a newborn giraffe and I bite back laughter as I crank the shower and we step under the spray.

After soaping each other up for longer than necessary, we rinse and towel off. I hand her a pair of my sweats and a T-shirt, and don the same.

I admit I never thought a woman would look sexy in my clothes, but fuck me running because I never want to see Peyton in anything *but* my clothes. None of it snug on her frame or exposing skin other than arms and above the collar.

Just damn.

Reaching out, I fist the shirt near her belly and tug her until our bodies are flush. Drop my lips to hers, clutch the back of her neck and kiss the hell out of her. Then cut the kiss short before I get carried away.

"Really need to leave the bedroom and feed you," I mutter, my lips still on hers.

Slender arms wrap around my waist and pin me to her. "Probably right. Although, I'd rather stay exactly where we are."

"Ugh," I huff out, grab her hand, and stumble out of the bedroom. "C'mon. Time to eat."

Peyton plops down on a stool at the breakfast bar as I get to work in the kitchen. I pull out all the ingredients for French toast, bacon, and sliced fruit. Within minutes, the scent of maple and cinnamon fill the room as I flip the bacon one last time and add the final pieces of French toast to the pan. When the last piece turns golden brown, I plate it, add fresh fruit and bacon on the side, and top the French toast with powdered sugar and whipped cream.

"A girl could get used to this," Peyton states as I set a plate in front of her and hit the brew button on the Keurig.

"Is that so?" I set down our coffees, park on the stool beside her and kiss her temple. "Good to know."

Breakfast with Peyton gives life a new definition of comfortable. With her, I am more at home than I have been in years. I don't second-guess myself or wonder what comes next. There are no absurd expectations or the need to be someone I am not.

With Peyton, I get to be myself. Not the guy who put up a front and bedded any willing woman because he felt empty and sad. I haven't been me in so long, haven't felt comfortable in my own skin with anyone else, and I love how she has guided the old me back into the light.

All too soon, our plates empty and Peyton prepares to head home before work. I don't let her change back into her clothes—the idea of her out in the world in my tee and sweats is a major turn-on.

"Talk to you later."

"Damn right you will," I say as I frame her face and kiss her one last time. "Have a good night at work, hellcat."

Peyton gets in her car, backs out, and drives off. I walk back into the house, go back to my room, and plop down on the bed. Hints of her coconut mint scent hit my nose and I close my eyes.

It may be too soon—what the hell do I know—but I more than like Peyton. But because I have been burned, I still fear the word that comes with the next level of emotion. So, I ignore the anxiety-inducing four-letter word and just think of her. The woman with golden hair and violet eyes. The woman who has bewitched me in every way possible.

Poorly sang rock music pierces my eardrums in an attempt to ruin yet another classic. As great of an idea as karaoke was for Roar, I may have to suggest some songs stay off the list of options. Peyton, on the other hand, snort-laughs her ass off next to Shelly and Cora. The sound equal parts disturbing and adorable as fuck.

My hand on Peyton's thigh under the table gives a gentle squeeze. Turning to face me, her laughter pauses a beat as my favorite smile lights her face. A smile that screams happiness and affection and gratitude. This single glance spreads heat through my chest. Gives me a sense of weightlessness. Fulfills me in an unfamiliar way, but one I don't want to end.

"You seem all too happy these people are trashing classic songs," I tease.

Peyton play smacks my bicep and shakes her head. "Not happy. Plus, I can forget their rendition, if I choose to. But c'mon." She waves a hand toward the stage. "You can't tell me this isn't hilarious to watch."

I narrow my eyes at her, then shift my gaze to the makeshift karaoke stage inside Roar. Karaoke always seems to bring in the oddest mix of people. Every age group and a wide array of music. Current and classic and everything in between. The man with the mic to his lips right now, he slaughters "Ramble On" by Led Zeppelin. Every muscle inside me cringes, but I suppose it is for entertainment.

"Whatever." I shrug. "Gonna go work in the office." I lean closer, so only she hears my next statement. "Join me in a bit."

"Yes." She inches back. "I'll hang here a bit longer, do rounds then be there."

Pressing a kiss to her temple, I rise from the chair and excuse myself. "See you guys later."

I don't rush to the office. My stride is a hair slower than usual as I nod and smile to patrons on the way. I make my way inside the office, shut the door, and drop down in the chair behind the desk. Get to work and don't fret over when Peyton will join me. Although most have inferred we are a couple, we don't need people believing either of us slacks off on the job.

In the middle of ordering, the door opens and in walks Peyton. Hair half up in a messy bun with the rest trailing down her back. Black dress slacks snug on her thighs, her sculpted ass partially visible under the tail of her mint-green top. A top that allows me an occasional view of her cleavage.

"How's it coming along in here?" Peyton asks as she saunters over.

"About done." I spin the chair to face her, lean back and tilt my head as I bite my bottom lip. "Things good out there?" I avert my gaze to the door momentarily with a nod.

"Mmhm." She braces herself on the chair arms, slips a leg between mine and closes the space between us.

When our lips meet, I sit up straighter. Snake my arms around her waist. Awkwardly lower her to my lap; the two of us a fumbling mess of limbs. She shifts her leg and scoots forward as I do the same. My hands slip up the back of her shirt and press her impossibly closer.

It would be so easy to strip her bare and take her on the desk. Swipe my arm across the oak and send paperwork flying. Fling pens to the floor and bend her over. Slap her ass and take her from behind. Press her cheek to the grain and tug the loose strands of her hair as I pummel her over and over.

God, would it be easy. Which is why I won't go through with it.

Much as I would love to fuck Peyton every waking minute of the day, we need rules. Rules that include behaving—minus the occasional kiss—at work. If rules aren't set, we will spend every Wednesday and Thursday in this office doing R-rated acts. Ani may be Peyton's friend, but she would not be too pleased to pay us to make out or fuck like horny teens on the clock.

I break the kiss and lean back into the chair. "We should work." The jut of her lower lip and batting lashes is adorable as hell. And damn, it begs me to break every rule put in place. "I'd much rather kiss you all night, but—and I can't believe I'm the one saying this—we should behave."

She leans back, a smirk on her lips and a knowing look in her eyes. "Who knew?"

My brows bunch together. "What?"

"That Micah Reed would choose to be the responsible one." She rises from my lap, gives me a chaste kiss and adjusts her top as she starts for the door. Twisting the knob, she stops and looks over her shoulder. "I like it." The corners of her mouth kick up. "A lot." Then she waltzes out the door and leaves me to finish the office work. Alone.

For a solid five minutes, I stare at the door. Not in the hopes she will walk through again. The opposite, actually. Because Peyton Alexander is nothing like I expected. She is next level. A commanding force, but also a woman who will submit when asked. An exquisite creature who captivates me at every turn. She keeps me on my toes and surprises me with each step forward we take. She has me dreaming of possibilities.

Of next steps and the years to come. With her.

FOURTEEN

PEYTON

Arriving at Roar early, I park beside Micah's truck with a wide-stretched smile on my face. Neither of us gets here early to do anything untoward. But the free time with no eyes on us is nice.

Before heading inside, I walk the short distance to the mailbox cluster for the plaza, unlock the club's postal box, and retrieve the mail. Thick stack of envelopes in hand, I hike my purse higher on my shoulder and enter through the employee door. Low-volume rock music plays from the speakers in the main room and floats down the hall. I drop the stack of mail and my purse on the desk and stroll out to the main area of the club.

Micah sets up the Bar Olympics, unaware of my presence. As I have on several occasions, I hang back at the edge of the hallway and watch him. Stare at his broad shoulders, thick arms, and dexterous fingers. Fingers that have clenched my throat and pinched my nipples. I swallow and drop my gaze to his trim waist and sculpted ass, snug in his slacks. An ass I have dug my nails into more than once. I lick my lips as he moves around with ease and an air of masculinity.

Oblivious to company, Micah is his true self. More laid back and effortless. Relaxed. No front or phony disposition. No flashy smiles or smart remarks. He is just… him.

And I love seeing this side of him. Love seeing him more himself. Quiet and focused and determined. It is a side not many get to see. Not even his family. I consider myself lucky I get the privilege.

"Gonna keep fawning over me?" he says, barely over the music, with his back to me.

Pushing off the wall, I walk in his direction. "What can I say? I was enjoying myself." When I reach him, he sets the red plastic cups down and grabs hold of my hip. "How long have you been here?"

I rest my forearms on his shoulders and toy with his hair. "Not long. You?"

"Maybe thirty minutes." He presses one, two, three chaste kisses to my lips.

Doing my best to behave, I don't push for more. I will save that for after hours. "Need help?"

He kisses the tip of my nose, then steps back. "Sure."

After the Olympics are set up, we both head to the office. Olympics night has become such a hit in the last few weeks, it ends up being an all-hands-on-deck-while-open event. Micah and I help out on the floor and behind the bar to keep the night flowing as smoothly as possible.

Micah shakes the mouse to wake up the computer as I start opening the mail. A few invoices and payments later, I come across an envelope addressed to Micah. There is a return address, but no company name.

"Here." I hold the envelope out in his direction. "This is addressed to you."

His forehead scrunches as his brows pull together. He takes the envelope and stares at the return address as if waiting for it to tell him the sender's name. After a moment, he flips it over and tears at the flap. Takes out a folded piece of paper and flattens it out. He scans the paper but doesn't move otherwise.

From where I stand, the words are unreadable. The typed letter appears brief with a printed logo on the top left.

Unable to bear the silence any longer, I speak up. "What is it?"

When he lifts his head and his starry eyes meet mine, I stop breathing. He looks as if he has seen a ghost. Skin gray, eyes dull, lips slightly parted. Frozen in fear.

Nausea rolls in my belly. Has me taking slow breaths and swallowing to settle the sensation. But until he answers, I know the feeling won't vanish.

"Micah?" I walk around the desk and touch his shoulder.

He holds up the letter for me to take. "It's from a clinic." I glance down at the paper. "To take a paternity test." Glassy eyes stare up at me in shock. His jaw shifts left to right, again and again. "Tomorrow."

Oh shit.

How long has it been since the woman in the red dress set foot in Roar and claimed Micah fathered the baby in her belly? More than a month. Hell, closer to two months have passed. Her silence hadn't made me forget her. But I had hoped she would take her accusation train somewhere else.

Who knows… maybe Micah was the easiest guy to pin down because she knew his workplace. Her other rendezvous may have been with random guys in clubs. And if no names were exchanged, she would have no way to find the *actual* father. Unfortunately for Micah, his job made him an easy target in this situation.

I take the paper from his hands and read it line by line.

Mr. Micah Reed:

This letter serves to notify you of a scheduled paternity test requested by Ms. Janine Vallons and her attorney, Kristin Montgomery, Esq.

The test will be performed at Life and Wellness Health Facility, Friday, August 5th at 12:00 p.m.

Please bring one form of government-issued identification and arrive at least thirty minutes prior to the appointment time listed to fill out paperwork.

Regards,

Life and Wellness Health Facility

"How the hell is it acceptable to give a person less than twenty-four hours' notice?" I bark out.

Micah keeps his eyes trained on the desk and doesn't say a word. I swipe the envelope up and look at the date stamp from the post office. Postmarked on Tuesday. Even if it arrived yesterday, the short notice is unprofessional and mind-boggling—especially by mail. I would love to give this facility a piece of my mind. But without knowing if it was them or the attorney acting through them, it would be uncouth of me to do so.

Frozen in place, Micah has yet to look up, react, or speak in regard to the situation. He needs time to process it all, but seeing him like this forms an empty pit in my stomach. But now is not the time to focus on how I feel. Now, I need to pour all my energy into Micah. Help him —us—get past this momentary road block.

Because we will get past it.

I comb my fingers through his hair—slow and gentle. Over and over, without a word spoken. Little by little, he leans into my touch. Closes his eyes, then slowly spins the chair until he faces me. Places a hand on my hip, then the other, and pulls me into him. Rests his forehead on my belly and draws in ragged breaths.

"Don't ask me how, but I *know* this baby isn't mine. But taking a test, having some lab run my DNA against an unborn baby's sample, terrifies me more than anything." His voice trembles as he hugs me closer.

Fingers still in his hair, I continue to comb through his locks and soothe him—and me—the best I can. "I believe you. This letter... anyone receiving this would be nervous as hell. But we'll get through this."

Slowly, he leans back and lifts his eyes until they hold mine prisoner. Red veins crowd the whites of his eyes. The usual sparkle in his irises is absent. "Will you go with me?" Tears well his eyes as he digs his fingers into my hips and awaits my answer.

Seems such a simple question to answer. A short word in response. Weeks ago, my first response would have probably been no. Or that I needed to think it over and get back to him. Not that there is much time, but the me from weeks ago would have made him wait. Possibly until hours before the appointment.

Now, Micah and I are different people. Apart and together. The dynamic of our relationship has changed. Leveled up. It holds power and strength and heart. Isn't solely based on attraction, but something more powerful. Hidden beneath the surface. Deeper. More profound. Something only he and I see and feel and grasp.

I frame his face with my hands. Brush my thumbs over the slight stubble on his cheeks. Hold his starry, constellation gaze. "Yes." I bend and press a kiss to his lips. "I'll go with you."

"Thank you," he whispers, then turns into my hand and kisses the center of my palm.

"Anytime." I press another kiss to his forehead. "Do you want to stay back here tonight? Or be on the floor?"

Unsure how his mood will be around others, I give Micah the option to choose. I would want the choice if our roles were reversed.

"If I stay in here, I'll drive myself mad."

"'Kay." I comb my fingers through his hair again. "Let's wrap things up in here and then we can both spend tonight on the floor. Sound good?"

"Perfect." He gives my hips one last squeeze, drops his hands and swivels back to face the desk. "And Peyton?"

"Yeah?"

"Thank you." I tilt my head at him. "For not running. For agreeing to go with me to the clinic."

I give him a small half smile. "You're welcome." I hold his eyes a beat longer. "Now, get to work, starlight."

"Yes, ma'am, hellcat."

FIFTEEN

MICAH

Fuck.

Can't hold the goddamn pen to save my life. But I will be damned if *Janine* sees my hand—or any other part of me—shake. Hell. No.

I stare down at the stack of papers trapped under the metal prong on the clipboard and lose focus. Zone out as the reality of what is happening hits harder. Black printed letters swirl in a sea of white and yellow and green sheets of paper. The letters jumble and spell new words. Words I refuse to believe until they are proven true.

I am not the father of this child. I am not the father of this child.

In thirty minutes, I have to let some unknown doctor or nurse stick an oversized cotton swab into my mouth and swipe it over the inside of my cheek. Take a sample of my DNA, seal it in a tube, and process it in some random lab to tell me whether or not I fathered an unborn baby.

I lift a loose fist to my lips, close my eyes, take a deep, shaky breath, and fight the bile creeping up my throat.

Then, the sensation subsides. Warmth radiates in my chest and settles every anxiety-ridden thought. I open my eyes and spy Peyton's hand on my thigh. Her thumb stroking back and forth, back and forth. The small motion and weight of her hand is exactly what I need. An elixir.

She leans in, her breath hot on my ear and soothing for my soul. "Want me to fill it out?"

Peyton doesn't ask because I appear incompetent. She asks because this is one of the most stressful circumstances in my adult life. Although I try to mask my difficulties, she sees the slight tremor in my limbs. The occasional bounce in my knee. Hears the slight hiccup in my breathing. Notices the fact I haven't brought pen to paper and filled out the documents yet.

And this amazing woman—one I am damn lucky to call mine—offers to help. Offers to be my strength when I fear I cannot be.

"No, I got it." I take a slow, deep breath. "Just don't move your hand. Please."

Once I finish the paperwork, which was way more involved than the basic questions a general practitioner asks, I hand it back to the man behind the reception counter and he returns my identification. Janine has yet to make an appearance, but I assume since she set all this up, she completed paperwork ahead of time.

Somewhere nearby, a clock second hand ticks softly behind the generic doctor waiting room music. A muted television plays a home renovation show. Disinfectant mixes with artificial rose air freshener and creates an unpleasant smell. And every five seconds, the man behind reception gives me a sad half smile.

The walls inch closer and my breath comes in short bursts. My nails bite the skin at the center of my palms and form deep crescent moons. I blink a few times as the room seems to bend and flex around me. The need to vomit and pass out hit me simultaneously as I break out in a cold sweat.

Can't say I remember being claustrophobic at any point in my life, but I feel trapped inside myself. Incapable of doing anything, of speaking up, of running away. Is that what claustrophobia feels like? Being a prisoner in your own skin?

"You okay?" Peyton whisper-asks.

I subtly shake my head. "Not so much."

She studies my face a beat. "Shit. You're pale. Don't move." She bolts from the chair and steps into the bathroom off the waiting area. Before the count of ten, she sits beside me and presses a cool, damp paper towel to the back of my neck. "Deep breaths," she whispers. "Close your eyes. I'm here. I got you."

I do as she suggests and close my eyes. Focus on my breathing and her hand at the back of my neck as the other draws small, lazy circles on my thigh. And it helps. Settles my heart rate and breathing. Calms my crazed thoughts of *what if*.

And Peyton is the key. The epicenter of tranquility. If

not for her, I would be passed out on the floor.

"Thank you," I say and lay a hand over hers. "Wouldn't be able to get through this without you."

She kisses my temple. "Glad you have me."

"Me too."

"Mr. Reed?" a shorter woman asks as she steps into the waiting area with a file folder clutched to her chest.

"Yes," I choke out. "That's me."

She gives a bright smile, one I am sure she reserves for clients. "If you'll come with me."

Looking at Peyton, I ask, "Can she come back too?"

"Yes." She nods to reaffirm. "She may join us."

We rise from our chairs and head for the door. Just as we reach it, the front door to the clinic office opens and in walks Janine. The first thing I notice is how *large* her belly is. Like way too big to be only roughly three months pregnant, but not quite third trimester pregnant.

But I don't have time to think on it as the woman in the white coat escorts us farther into the lab.

The first thing I notice as we walk down a corridor is how sterile this place looks and feels. Not that doctor offices don't typically appear neat and hygienic, but this place is next level. Bare white walls—no generic health posters in cheap frames or doctorate degrees. Shiny light-gray linoleum floors that reflect the fluorescent lighting and squeak if you stub your shoe sole. And the antiseptic smell... the stinging smell ten times worse back here than the waiting room.

White coat lady leads us into a small room off the hall

and directs me to sit on the exam table. Peyton sits in a chair off to the side and remains quiet as the woman explains the process.

"Mr. Reed, the procedure to collect your DNA sample is simple and painless." She points to a paper-lined tray on a rolling cart where sealed tubes and packaged cotton swabs wait to be used. "This tube is labeled with a barcode matching that in our file." She opens my file, then holds up the tube and shows me the matching barcodes. "This is to protect your sample once it goes to processing. Your name will not appear on anything, which keeps the test confidential. After processing, your DNA sample is then destroyed." She sets the tube back on the tray and closes the file. Then points to the sealed cotton swab. "The sterile swab will be used to catch saliva and cells from your cheek. Then it is placed in the tube and a new seal is placed on the sample. Do you have any questions before I collect the sample?"

The test seems pretty straightforward and noninvasive. I expected needles and hair plucking and skin scraping until I searched the web last night. When I learned a ball of cotton on a long stick would be rubbed along the inside of my cheek, I questioned the testing system. Seems too easy. To swipe someone's cheek to learn their internal fingerprint.

"How long will the results take?" I ask.

This is the biggest question of all. First and foremost—gut instinct told me from the start, this baby isn't mine. Second—seeing the size of Janine's belly when she walked into the clinic, instinct went into hyperdrive. The sooner I have the results, the sooner this clinic confirms what I know deep in my soul, the sooner this whole debacle will be over.

And although I swear the outcome will swing in my favor, it doesn't stop the constant, violent buzz from the hornet's nest inside my rib cage.

"Test results typically come back in two to five days, depending on how busy the lab is. With the pregnancy at nineteen weeks, the sample from the mother is easier to attain. As soon as the results are available, we send them to the email address you listed as well as a physical copy via postal mail. Any other questions?"

I shake my head. "No, ma'am." But I do stash the pregnancy time frame away for further thought.

"Very good."

The tech or nurse or doctor—whatever she is—walks over to the small sink and sets the file on the counter before washing her hands. She resumes her position in front of me and goes through a routine she probably does dozens of times per day.

She picks up glove one and works her hand into it. Sweat pricks my forehead and temples.

Repeats the process for glove two. A drop of sweat rolls down my temple and lodges itself in the stubble I have yet to shave.

She breaks the seal on the tube and sets the stopper on the tray. I swallow in an effort to rid the lump in my throat.

Next, she peels open the cotton swab package and removes the largest Q-Tip I have ever seen. My pulse whooshes loud and fast and hard in my ears.

"Open your mouth as wide as possible, please," she instructs.

I follow her instructions and avert my gaze to the ceiling. Bad enough I have to do this, but to witness the process… no thanks. Seconds that mirror centuries pass as the cotton wad scrapes and swirls and gathers from my cheek. My fingers curl into fists as my breathing escalates. I work to focus on anything except the fibrous material collecting my cells.

"All done," the woman states. My eyes open and I watch as she places the swab in the tube, replaces the stopper, peels a red strip off a paper and seals it around the tube and stopper. "This sticker assures your sample is not contaminated before processing. If the sample gets opened, this sticker separates and lets the technician know the sample has been opened and compromised."

She peels the gloves away, tosses them in the red biohazardous waste bin and washes her hands again. She dries her hands with paper towels, tosses them in the bin, collects my patient file and sample, then guides us to the door.

"One last stop before you leave," she states. "If you'll follow me."

We continue down the corridor and stop another twenty feet down beside a smoky sliding window. She knocks on the window and a moment later, it slides open.

"Afternoon, Becca," a man says with a smile.

"Hey, Frank. Sample drop off."

My eyes remain locked on the long tube as she hands it over to the man. He takes it and tosses me a cordial smile. Before another word is spoken, the tube disappears from view and the window shuts.

"You're all set. Let me walk you out to the front." The woman steps in front and leads us to the waiting area door.

Peyton laces her fingers with mine and gives them a squeeze. I glance her way, take in her subtle smile and gentle eyes. How she studies me, reads the words I don't speak aloud. I soak up her quiet strength and tenacious affection. An affection I never expected to receive, but will cherish every day I have it.

No one occupies the waiting room when we step out. The receptionist confirms my email and mailing address and phone number one last time before we leave. He reiterates how and when I will receive the results. Then we leave.

"Hungry?" Peyton asks as she drives us out of the lot.

"Yes and no. Probably should eat."

"I'll find somewhere closer to the house."

For a beat, a small sliver of my brain focuses on how Peyton said *the* house and not *your* house. Call my thought process juvenile, I don't give a fuck, but small differences like that do crazy things to my heart.

Unfortunately, all happy thoughts leave my head as I

recycle what just happened at the clinic. Hundreds of what-if questions cycle through my mind. Questions that have no resolute answer until the results hit my inbox. Of course, I can speculate where all this will lead, but without answers, it isn't worth expending the energy or torturing myself.

Then, I recall something else. *"With the pregnancy at nineteen weeks, the sample from the mother is easier to attain."* Nineteen weeks. Nineteen. Weeks. What is that in months? Just shy of five, and half the normal gestation period of human pregnancy.

Five months seems like too long.

Two months have passed since she came into Roar with her announcement. Call me crazy, or ignorant, but don't most women have some sign or symptom of pregnancy within a month or so? If she is nineteen weeks, that means she was roughly eleven weeks along when she spoke up. Which makes no sense whatsoever.

I think back to months ago. Run through the faces of women I went to bed with and when. A not-so-simple task since I slept with dozens of women in the months leading up to me and Peyton. The moment sparks flew between us, the moment I thought it possible to have more with Peyton, I refused to be with another woman.

When I finally recall Janine's face, my eyes go wide. She was literally one of the last few women I slept with before cutting myself off. At the end of April.

"This baby isn't mine," I say over the radio.

Peyton pats my thigh before leaving her hand there. "I

hope that's true, but we won't know until the results are back."

I turn in the passenger seat to face her and all but slice my throat with the seat belt. After I adjust the belt, I continue my thought. My voice stronger, louder, bolder this time. "No. I mean, there is no possible way this baby is mine."

Peyton takes her eyes off the road a split second to narrow them at me. "How can you be so sure?"

I lay my hand over hers and take a cleansing breath. "The person who took my sample, she said Janine is nineteen weeks."

"Yeah, so?"

"Since the letter yesterday, I've been in my head a lot. One thing I remembered…" I pause for a beat and take a deep breath. "…is when I was with her. Yes, I have been with a lot of women, but I don't forget a face. Ever. And I've been thinking about it, really thinking about it, since that woman said nineteen weeks."

I stare out the driver's side window. Take in the Bay as the sun glistens on the water. Stare after the seagulls as they fight over scraps from an unlidded trash bin. For the first time in less than twenty-four hours, a sense of relief washes over me.

"And? Don't leave me hanging."

"I was with her near the end of April. Fourteen, maybe fifteen weeks ago. Tops. Just before I stopped hooking up."

"You mean, before there was potential for us."

"Yes." I wrap her hand with my own. "Even if the chances were slim, I didn't want to fuck up the opportunity." I lift her hand and kiss her knuckles. "So, without a doubt, I *know* this baby isn't mine."

"Why do you think she came to you then?"

I shrug. "Was probably the easiest person to find. She knew where I worked. If she hooked up with random strangers in clubs or bars, chances are she has no way to find them. Not unless they exchanged numbers or hooked up at the other person's house."

"Are you sure you're remembering the correct person at the correct time?" She peers over from the driver's seat, a smirk on her lips. "You do have a thing for blondes. No doubt they all blend together." Her tone is teasing, but I get her meaning.

With my free hand, I reach over, pinch a strand of her champagne locks between my fingers, and give a slight tug. "Blondes have more fun. I should know, I am one."

"Ha ha." She makes a silly face, but I only catch her profile.

I twirl her hair around a finger and simply watch her as she drives. Can't recall a time in my life where a woman has made me so introspective. Has made me really dig deep and see past the mundane. Has made me want more from life—not because that is what I should do, but because I want more with her.

"Or maybe I wanted one specific blonde and the others were mental distractions."

We reach a red light and she faces me. "What?" She

appears genuinely confused by my admission.

"Peyton, it's no secret I pined for you from the beginning. Even the days when you verbally bit my head off, I still wanted you." Laughter vibrates my chest. "For so long, I never knew why you despised me from the get-go. At first, I thought it was your form of banter. But soon realized it wasn't. I didn't want to give up, though."

The light turns green and she faces the road again. We remain quiet the rest of the drive until Peyton parks at a delicatessen near the house. The restaurant somewhat busy considering the time of day.

Unbuckling her belt, she twists to face me fully. I mimic the action, and for a moment, we just sit and stare at each other. Her violet irises hidden behind dark lenses as she holds my gaze. With some, I would shake off their nonstop gaze. But with Peyton, I want her eyes on me as often as possible. Want the attention she gives and the radiance it generates just beneath my sternum and to the left.

"Glad you didn't," she says.

Glad I didn't what? I scrunch my brow. "What?"

"Give up. I'm glad you didn't."

For three breaths, I sit immobile. Then I lean across the console, wrap my hand around the back of her neck, pull her close, and kiss the hell out of her. We make out like teenagers in the parking lot for several minutes. I don't know who breaks the kiss, but I press my forehead to hers when it ends.

"Me too, hellcat. Me too."

SIXTEEN
PEYTON

ROLLING OVER, I curl into Micah's side. Breathe in the scent of him; a faint hint of his cologne mixed with a scent distinct to Micah. Bask in his warmth and comfort, and snuggle his frame. He curls an arm around my waist, hugs me impossibly closer, and eliminates all space between us. Then he kisses the top of my head and I sigh and kiss his shoulder.

"Morning." His raspy tone wakes up more than my mind.

Throwing a leg over his hips, I roll to straddle him and press my breasts into his chest. "Morning."

Since Sunday evening, after hanging out at Autumn and Jonas's place, I have spent every night in Micah's bed. Woken up the next morning with our limbs twisted in new pretzel shapes. Been pummeled by or ridden on his dick after we say good morning. Dug my nails into his skin and bruised it with my lips.

And each morning after we come, I want him again. In the shower. On the couch or kitchen counter or dining table. Against the glass wall facing the backyard. Out back on the veranda. Wherever I can have him. His head between my legs or me on my knees in front of him or both our mouths on each other.

Micah Reed makes me insatiable. A wanton creature. For him, and only him.

How many times per day is considered abnormal? Is too much sex unhealthy? I would think not, but I am no sex therapist. All I know is I have never felt so damn good in my life.

I bury my nails in his pecs. Mark my ownership of him next to the previous marks, now fading. Rock my hips harder as he holds on to them and jerks up into me over and over. The delicious rhythm drives me higher and higher. I tip my head back, hair tickling my tailbone as I close my eyes and gasp at the ceiling. He rams into me as I slam down on him.

Familiar, delicious heat builds low in my abdomen. Spirals up, up, up until it hits between my breasts and disperses like wildfire. Fire crawls up my chest, my neck, my face. My eyes roll back in my head. Panted high-pitch whimpers and throaty grunts ricochet off the walls. The animalistic scent of sex drifts through the air. My body starts to constrict Micah's cock. He clamps down on my nipples—hard—and tugs with a twist.

I sink my nails deeper and shatter around him. My body exhausted yet eager for more. He flips me on my back and pistons hard and fast. The headboard smacks the wall as skin slaps skin. He bruises my thighs with his fingers. Slides a hand up my abdomen, my breast and stops at my throat. His thumb, third and fourth fingers clamp down, making me dizzy and euphoric.

Slap. Slap. Slap.

Stars fill my vision, my breaths come in short bursts, and my body constricts his once more. Micah growls into my neck, crushes my pelvis with his, and releases inside me.

His arms buckle and he gives me his full weight. And I welcome it. Wrap my legs around his waist and arms around his chest. Bear-hug him to my chest and breathe in the scent of our sweat and orgasms. Trace my fingers up his spine and over his scalp.

"Never want to wake up without you," he mumbles into the crook of my neck.

I freeze at his words. Not because they frighten me or make me want to bolt. Quite the opposite, actually. A lightness I have never experienced with anyone slips into my bloodstream. Consumes me. Fashions a new energy in the chambers of my heart and pumps it through my veins. Warms me in ways I never thought possible.

My limbs relax and I comb my fingers through his hair. "Me either."

He kisses up my neck, sucks the sensitive spot beneath my ear, then kisses his way to my lips. "C'mon." He pushes up and scoots off the bed. "Let's shower, then eat." Standing at the foot of the bed, he grabs my ankles and yanks me down. Me and the bedding plummet to the floor and I erupt in a fit of laughter.

When I gain control, I sit eye level with his cock. His not-so-soft cock. I lift my gaze to his and lick my lips.

"Hellcat…" he says in warning. "Shower." I push out my lower lip and aim for my saddest puppy eyes. He growls. "Now." He offers his hand and I take it.

"Fine," I say on a huff, then stomp off to the bathroom.

Little does he know, I have tricks up my invisible sleeve.

By the time we step out of the shower, our skin is wrinkly and legs wobbly. But damn, do I feel like a queen. Micah definitely makes a great devotee and king.

We move around the kitchen like an old married couple. He whips up eggs, sausage, home fries, and toast while I cut fruit and brew coffee. His task seems more daunting, but it works for us. In no time, we plate up food and sit at the bar to eat.

We push food around our plate more than eat it. Forks scraping the ceramic, occasional chewing, and coffee slurps are the only sounds in the room. Breakfast came out perfect… we just don't have the oomph to enjoy it.

Today is day five. Five treacherous, unbearable days have passed.

And although I haven't seen him on his phone this morning, Micah has probably checked his email several times. Which means nothing has arrived yet. If it had, whatever the result, I would be the first to know—after him, of course.

We finish breakfast in amicable silence, then plop down on the couch and watch a movie until it is time to dress for work. Arms wrapped around each other, we cuddle on the couch and do our best to not pick at our nails or tap our fingers with unreleased nervous energy.

But every now and then, Micah's knee bounces or his breathing picks up. He tries to not let it show, but I notice. I just keep it to myself.

The movie ends and we amble to the bedroom to dress for work. We move slower than usual, but it isn't long before we head for the door. Since I have stayed with Micah the past few nights, we decide to take one car to work on the days we both go in. Why waste the gas?

In this very moment, driving together works out in our favor.

His phone alerts him to an incoming email as we slip into my SUV. He opens the message after buckling his belt. All I can do is stare and wait while he reads the screen.

How can five seconds feel like five years? My heart beats out of my chest as I wait for some reaction from him. The downturn of his lips. A smile worthy of conquering the world. Anything.

Finally, he breaks the silence.

"Hell yeah!" he screams in the confines of the car. "Woo!" His whole body vibrates as the biggest smile I have ever seen brightens his face.

This has to be good news for him. Please let it be good news.

"Not a match?" I ask, just to be certain.

"There is zero probability that the donor tested has any familial relationship," he reads from the email, then faces me. "Zero. Zilch. Nada. I knew it! I fucking knew it!"

Thank goodness I hadn't backed us out of the driveway yet. Micah bounces around like a kid high on too much Halloween candy. No way in hell I would be able to focus on the road with his excitement. Not to mention my own.

Relief I never knew possible hits me like a summer downpour. *Zero probability. No familial relationship.* The sudden weightlessness exhilarates and consoles me. *Jesus.* I didn't realize how badly I needed to hear those words.

Not that I wouldn't have stood by Micah's side if the opposite result was delivered. But this... happy and relaxed are a microscopic percentage of the elation I feel right now.

I unbuckle my belt, claw across the console for him, haul him to me and hug the hell out of him.

"Deep down, I knew it too. Glad the results finally came and were what we thought and hoped they would be."

Strong arms hold me close. "Just glad this is over and we can put it behind us now."

"Me too."

Micah leans back enough to look me in the eye. "We should go, but..." He waggles his brows, his radiant smile still firmly in place. "We are definitely celebrating later."

"Celebrating, huh? And what exactly did you have in mind?"

He shrugs. "Hadn't gotten that far yet. Still have plenty of time to figure that part out."

After I buckle my belt again, I back out of the driveway and head toward Tampa. Micah cranks up the music and sings obnoxiously with the songs on the radio. From the corner of my eye, I watch him every chance I get.

I love his new ease and cheery disposition. The endless smile highlighting his sharp jaw. The additional sparkle in his starry eyes. The happy-go-lucky attitude emanating from him.

I am beyond glad this whole fiasco with the red-dress woman will soon become a distant memory. One we will have no problem erasing.

Now… it is time to build new memories. Better ones to replace all the bad. And I am eager to get started.

SEVENTEEN

MICAH

ALL STRESS LEFT my body after reading that email. An email I plan to print and stash in the miscellaneous file for years to come. Not that I think Janine will try to pull something in the future. More as a reminder of my idiotic past choices and how they could have ruined what continues to bloom between me and Peyton.

Nothing will ruin what I have with Peyton.

My face hurts from the smile that won't fade. But I will take the pain and smile twice as hard. Brighten the world with my pearly teeth and endless exuberance. This pain is the best pain. And later tonight, I don't care what we do, but we sure as fuck will celebrate.

Peyton pulls into a space behind Roar. Soon as she throws the car in park, I whip off my belt, frame her face with my hands, and kiss the hell out of her. Kiss her until we both gasp for breath. She whimpers as the kiss breaks and it only makes my smile stretch wider.

I love how I leave her wanting more. Love how difficult it will be to resist temptation all night. Most of all, I love how it leads into the best seven-plus hours of foreplay. By the time we get home, her need for me will be ravenous. Even then, I may drag it out a bit longer.

"You head in. I'll get the mail," I say, then smack her ass.

"Best watch yourself, Reed." The way my last name rolls off my tongue does crazy things to my body.

"Yeah? Why's that, hellcat?"

"You're not the only one who likes to play games." Her lips kick up in a devious half smile, and then she winks. "See you inside." She disappears inside Roar and leaves me standing in the lot, bedazzled and horny.

After fetching the mail, I head inside. Peyton has parked herself behind the desk and works on all the monotonous tasks. So, I head out to the main part of the club and prep for Karaoke Night.

Time flies faster than usual and soon the rest of the staff arrives, does their prep work, and we unlock the doors for the evening. Drinks get mixed and poured. Horrible renditions of songs I love get belted out. And my favorite group of people walks through the front door.

Although karaoke had never been a favorite pastime, I love that I see Shelly and my friends more than once a week now. Love that I have a chance to sit with them and catch up more often. With my odd work hours, it hasn't always been easy to hang out.

Before long, Shelly and Cora skip off the stage after

their third song. Everyone finishes their drinks, exchanges hugs, and says they will see us Sunday.

Last call is announced and the Wednesday crowd starts to thin. A few patrons linger to slam one more glass before calling it a night. The staff shuffles around the club and rushes to complete their end-of-night duties. Minutes later, the front doors lock and we clean up faster than any previous night. One by one, the staff clocks out and heads home. In less than thirty minutes, Peyton and I do the same.

"Food from the diner near the house?" I toss out.

"Sounds good. Maybe we can grab dessert too."

It is on the tip of my tongue to tell her *she* is the only dessert I want. But I resist the urge and think of what I may do with said dessert. "Yeah, sure."

I place an order online for burgers, fries, milkshakes, and half a peanut butter pie from the diner near the house. We drive across the Bay with the windows down and the music loud. Salty air licks our skin and whips our hair. Our fingers laced over the center console and thumbs brushing the other's hand.

This right here... this is perfect.

Some of the simplest things in life are the most notable. Like a lover's hand in your own. Listening to them sing with the radio as you drive down the highway. The glimmer in their eye when they give you a side-glance and smile. Those small details are ones I deem most precious. I hug them close to my heart and don't take them for granted.

Lost in thoughts of us, I miss the moment Peyton pulls into the diner parking lot. Miss her pull into a space and put the car in park. But I don't miss her laugh when she looks over at me with raised brows and wide eyes.

"You want me to get the food?"

I break contact with her and stare out the windshield. Bright neon lights spell out *open* in red as the smell of fryer grease hits my nose.

"Oh. No, I got it," I fumble over my words as I unbuckle and exit the car.

In and out of the diner in less than a minute, we head back to the house with growling stomachs. Peyton parks behind my truck and I scoop up the bags. We amble to the front door, hand in hand, without a worry in the world.

We drop down on the couch and I take the food out of the bag, depositing take-out boxes on the table. She moves beside me as she has every night for weeks. And then it hits me. A new version of contentment. The ease at which Peyton and I have fallen into this new routine. Eating dinner on the couch with our legs crossed and knees bumping. Watching movies and television shows together as she curls into my side. Kissing and groping until we land in the sheets and sweat and moan our way toward ecstasy.

And I hope to do this every night and day with her in the future. Enjoy the simple moments. Like a shared meal or making breakfast together. Merge our lives. Become something bigger than who we are individually. Discover a new way to exist together. Find a happiness no one can dull. A happiness brighter than any star in the galaxy.

I finish my burger, set my empty take-out box on the table beside hers, hit pause on the show, then pull her onto my lap and hug her close. Peyton combs her fingers through my hair as I tip my head back and close my eyes. Being like this with her—vulnerable and more myself than ever—is the most freeing moment in my life.

Yes, I want to tear her clothes off and taste every inch of her right now. But the intimacy in this moment—her fingers lazy in my hair, eyes heating my skin, her coconut mint scent in the air, breath inches from my lips—I want it just as bad.

Intimacy without sex is somewhat new in my life. And I never knew how amazing it could be.

Her weight shifts and the heat of her breath hits my lips a beat before our lips connect. The kiss light at first. A tender graze of soft warmth. Her fingers stop in my hair and lightly tug on the strands as the kiss takes a gradual turn. From sweet and subtle to exploratory and eager to desperate and ravenous.

My hands at her knees inch up her thighs without hurry. The inclination to map her body, memorize every peak and path and adventure it takes me on, overwhelms me. To learn every perfection and imperfection and love them equally. To chart her freckles and name them like constellations. Discover each scar and kiss away any pain they cause.

Sex with Peyton is indescribable. Unlike any experience I had with another person. It isn't just the physicality. Being with Peyton... yes, what we share is raw and primal, deep and carnal. But it is also impeccable and disorienting, covetous and euphoric. Our bond makes me weak in the knees. Light-headed and unsteady.

With Peyton, I don't just picture the physical endgame when we have sex. I envision where it will lead us years from now. Sharing the same bed, day in and out. Not just for sex. I picture her limbs tangled with mine. Breath steady on my chest and palm over my heart. Hair splayed on my shoulder and the pillow. Breasts and hips snug to my side.

"Take me to bed," she whispers against my lips, then kisses me softly.

I snake my arms around her waist. "Hold on tight."

Peyton laces her fingers behind my neck. Scooting to the couch edge, I rise and walk us to the bedroom, her ankles locked at my lower back. Every step forward, she kisses my lips, my chin, the line of my jaw. Nips the lobe of my ear. Sucks the spot just above the pulse in my neck.

Every step forward is a match to the fuse only Peyton lights. One she sparks with her heady touch and reverent kisses. Fire and vibrancy and undiluted need spills from my veins. Every nerve ending wakes and begs for more. And deep in my marrow, my soul connects with hers.

The sensation engulfs me. Swallows me whole with no promise to let go.

And I never want it to let go.

I lay her on the bed. Kiss her as if she may crumble at

my touch. Unhook her feet and peel away her clothes. Then my own.

Skin to skin, the world around us disappears. For the next several hours, we connect like never before. Slow and sentimental, as if we have been lovers for a lifetime and not weeks. Every touch is special and new and incomparable to any previous connection we shared.

And when we curl into each other, breathless and sweaty and sated, an imaginary bulb lights in my head.

For the first time, I made love to a woman. Linked myself to her. Connected with her on the most intimate level. Bonded beyond the physical. Something I have never done. At this realization, a sense of wholeness engulfs me. Aligns all the little pieces that never fit right with anyone else.

Peyton does this. Straightens all the jagged edges and fixes all the broken parts. Without effort, Peyton makes me whole. Better. A man.

I squeeze her closer to my side, kiss the crown of her head and resist saying the three small words on the tip of my tongue. Words I have never said to any woman. Words I won't be able to resist saying much longer.

Question is… will Peyton reciprocate? Or has my love for her blinded me?

EIGHTEEN

PEYTON

HOOTS AND HOLLERS mingle with the cacophony of hundreds having conversations. Ping-Pong balls and red plastic cups slap tables. Quarters bounce to the floor. Stacked, precut two-by-fours, grow taller with each move and threaten to teeter.

Bar Olympics night is in full swing. Body odor and upbeat music fill the air. People stand on the sidelines and cheer on the players.

Smaller tables host card games or tic-tac-toe with shots. Bowls of peanuts and pretzels on every other table. While most people here play, several just drink and enjoy watching the festivities. Games aren't tracked via Roar, but most of the regulars make note of who leads who in the different games.

In the last two weeks, Ani and Sean hired more staff for Thursday, Friday, and Saturday. Roar has definitely had an uptick in patronage and sales since the changes took place. At first, the newer crowd was easily handled with the current crew. But not long after, it stressed out the former staff. Now, everyone smiles and goes about business as Ani and Sean envisioned—giving time to the customers and engaging with them so they will return. A win-win.

"One more hour," Micah says as he presses flush to my back, squeezes my hips, and kisses the spot beneath my ear.

"Mmm. Did you have something in mind for when said hour ends? Cause we still have to clean up."

His chest vibrates as a groan spills from his lips. "Several things we shouldn't do here." He kisses my neck and steps back as I spin to face him. "Let's get an early jump on cleaning, so we aren't stuck here all night. Then…" He pauses and stares as if he has something to say but isn't sure. "Maybe we can stay at your place tonight."

Stay at my place? Micah has a quiet, cozy house with no roommate. Why on earth would he want to stay in my tiny two-bedroom apartment with my best friend slash roommate? Not sure why, but it strikes me as odd.

"Something wrong at your house?"

He shakes his head. "No. Thought it'd be nice to experience your bed for once."

He wants to *experience* my bed? What does that mean? My imagination wanders in a blink and I picture Micah jumping on my bed like a child. Compared to his king-size bed, my full will be quite the *experience*. As in, snug and sweltering and a fight for covers.

But, whatever. If Micah wants to *experience* my bed, then that is what we will do.

"Sure thing. We'll pick up food on the way. Haven't grocery shopped since I've been staying at your place."

His lips press to my forehead a second before he smacks my ass. "Now, get to work, hellcat. Don't want to be here all night."

Micah saunters off as Kaylynn approaches with a blinding smile. An all-too-eager smile with dozens of questions. Questions I will *not* answer at work.

Kaylynn and I have been acquaintances from day one. But that is it. We never did anything outside these walls. Not because neither of us wanted to; it never came up. And now, I am her boss. Although we still behave somewhat the same around each other, there are boundaries we shouldn't cross. Boundaries *I* crossed before my promotion. But Ani was aware the entire time.

"Hey, girl," Kaylynn says as she sidles up beside me. "So, you and Micah, huh?"

"Mmhm," I mumble, loud enough for her to hear. Grabbing the clipboard beneath the bar top, I inventory what bottles and beers need to be brought from the storage room.

Less than a foot away, Kaylynn vibrates with curiosity. She has never been one to gossip, but I have never been one to spill my private life to people I don't know well. Yes, we have worked together for more than a year. But... I don't really *know* Kaylynn.

Is she single? Married? Divorced? Straight or bi or

lesbian? Does she have children or pets? They are all basic questions, but I don't know the answer to any of them. To be honest, I have no intention of asking either. Unless it is generic conversation and not one where we take mental notes of what shampoo we use and what happens behind closed doors.

Because that is where the conversation seems to be headed.

"How long? And how... is it?"

Micah and I have been hanging out for weeks. Hell, two months plus have passed since the first night I went to his house. But it wasn't until this past weekend, a few days after he made love to me for the first time, that we slapped a title on our relationship. That we dubbed each other boyfriend and girlfriend. Granted, we had been in the role already, we just hadn't given it a name.

But with the direction of our relationship, we figured, why not? In all ways, we fulfilled the role. Why not give the title to everyone who asked?

"For a while. Things are great."

The second half of my response left intentionally vague. She didn't outright ask anything specific. All aspects of our relationship are great, so the answer isn't false.

As she opens her mouth to ask another question, a customer steps up to the bar and distracts her. I take the opportunity to walk off under the guise of restocking the bar.

Down the hall, I unlock and enter the storage room

across from the office. On the opposite side of the hall, the office and employee lounge divide the space. The storage room, though, takes up the whole length and is roughly twice as deep.

Everything is organized by type, brand, and what sells faster. Beer fills more than half the space with kegs and cased bottles stacked high. Liquor sits on industrial shelves in rows. Paper goods, glassware and miscellaneous shelf-stable goods fill the remainder of the room.

I grab the items jotted down and set them on a rolling cart we keep for larger restocks. Exiting storage, I lock up and push the cart slower than necessary. Not because it has an overabundance of glass or weighs a lot. More because I want to creep out and locate Kaylynn before she does me.

Peering around the corner, I spot her wiping down the bar. With her back to me. As I round the corner, cart in tow, she reaches for the broom and gets to work on the floors.

Thank god.

Kaylynn is nice. Probably had no ill-meaning behind her inquisition. But I hate being in the position to say *no, I don't want to share my life with you.* Especially with someone who I have somewhat known a little more than a year.

Micah locks the door after the last person leaves. One pro Monday through Thursday… we close early. Much as I love the energy in those late-night hours on Friday and Saturday, I don't miss the exhaustion it brings. Yes, I miss the upbeat tempo and bass vibrating my bones. But not much else. If Micah and I still worked Friday and Saturday together, it wouldn't be like the other days. We would both be too busy to stop and say hello, much less wave across the packed club.

Kaylynn finishes the last of her cleanup as Micah and I stash the Bar Olympics tables in the storage room. We wave her off and do one last sweep of the bar and club before leaving.

I shoulder my purse while Micah shuts off the lights. We walk out, hop in my car and drive toward home.

"Stop by the house so I can grab some clothes."

"Sure. What sounds good to eat?"

At the mention of food, Micah quiets for a moment. His focus out the passenger window with his chin resting on a loose fist. From my vantage point, he appears too serious to be weighing food options.

On our side of the Bay, less than a mile from the house, he speaks up. His voice more reserved than usual.

"Sorry. Was just thinking."

"About?"

"This Sunday is family dinner night."

"Okay." I drag out the second syllable.

"And..." He tucks his lips between his teeth, swallows, then meets my gaze. "Mom wants me to bring you." My eyes widen briefly. "But please don't feel pressured to come if you don't want to," he adds quickly.

Have we reached this point in our relationship? Hell, less than a week has passed since we officially declared ourselves a couple. Does official status equal meeting the parents?

A thin layer of sweat blankets me and makes my clothes cling to my skin. White noise blocks my hearing as my heart pounds harder with each beat. My knuckles whiten as I fist the steering wheel.

Thank god we reach his house without me running a light or rear-ending someone.

I don't *think* it is his parents that have my nerves bouncing like live wires. But the step of meeting family is *huge*. It screams the legitimacy of our relationship. That I am no fluke. That Micah plans to have me around for weeks and months, and possibly years, to come.

Don't get me wrong, I love that he feels this way toward me. That I am not a random woman in his bed. He pictures more for us in the future. He *wants* there to be a future.

Me from a year ago—hell, four months ago—would laugh at the idea of a steady, solid relationship with Micah Reed.

Me today… she smiles painfully big.

Meeting the parents is a big deal, but we have overcome so much in the last three months. If I found a way to forgive Micah for his past discretions, I can swallow my nerves and join his family for dinner.

I pull into his driveway, throw the car in park, and shut off the engine. Since he said his parents wanted me to join family dinner, Micah has sat deathly quiet with his eyes on my profile. And I am grateful he allowed me a moment to digest the request without interruption.

"Dinner on Sunday would be nice," I say as I twist to face him.

His bright smile I love makes an appearance as he leans forward and kisses me. "Are you sure?" I nod. "Okay. We'll talk more about it later. For now, I want to grab clothes, my toothbrush, then some food." He plants a chaste kiss on my lips, then exits the car.

Once he has everything, we drive off and stop at the Chinese restaurant near my place. It is one of the few places that has late hours. One massive bag of noodles, rice, veggies, and meat later, I drive to my apartment.

As I park in front of the building, it dawns on me I didn't warn Reese. Not that an actual warning is necessary. More like I don't want us walking in the door and interrupting anything. Seeing as I haven't been at the apartment much in the last week or two, Reese has probably had his boyfriend over more. And neither of them understands quiet, if you catch my drift.

Like someone on the prowl, I creep up to the door, slowly insert my key and twist even slower. Micah looks at me as if I have lost my mind. I don't care, though. Twisting the knob, I tiptoe inside and listen for any sounds of fornication.

Micah chuckles behind me. "Will you just go." He taps my ass. "No one will jump out and grab us."

I slap the air behind me, straighten my spine, and step

out of the way for Micah to enter. "Sorry. Just wanted to make sure the couch wasn't occupied."

Leading Micah to the kitchen, he sets down the food and his overnight bag. His brows pinch together at the same time his lips pucker. "Does that usually happen? Your roommate having sex on the couch."

His ears must have been ringing because, as Micah finishes speaking, Reese strolls into the kitchen. With no shirt on. And sweat dripping down his abdomen.

"Who's having sex on the couch?" he asks and my cheeks heat.

"No one. Working out?" I ask and pray that was what he was doing.

"Sure." He smiles, then chuckles. "All done now, though." His eyes land on the bag of food. "Did you happen to get *me* dinner? I did just burn a shit ton of calories."

I slap his bicep. "Ew! Shut up. And yes, I got you orange chicken."

Reese hugs me against his sweaty chest. "You're the best." I shove him off with a laugh and he steps toward Micah with his hand extended. "We haven't been formally introduced. Reese."

Micah takes his hand and they shake. "Micah, but I'm sure you already know all about me." This time, they both laugh.

"Wouldn't say I know *all*, but quite a bit."

A moment of awkward silence passes and I beg for someone, anyone, to swoop in and make it end. Thankfully, Reese says he needs to wash up. He also asks if I mind his guest joining us. Of course, I agree and tease him about working out again.

We plate up food and get comfortable on the couch. After we select the next episode of *Peaky Blinders*, Reese and his new beau, Trent, join us.

The next hour is more normal than I imagined it would be. We all laugh and gasp at the same parts as we eat dinner. When the episode ends, we clean up, say our good nights and go to our rooms.

It isn't until we step foot in my room and I watch Micah's expression morph that I laugh. My room isn't girly or dirty or cluttered. But the bed is small. Way smaller than his. Literally half the size. In his defense, I didn't really warn him because I thought it would be fun.

"Great for cuddling," I say, his eyes still zoned in on the bed. "Best way to get closer. Don't you think?"

He laughs with a shake of his head. "I can think of other ways to get closer."

"Oh, really?"

"Mmhm. Come here." He curls his finger in a come-hither motion. "Let's see exactly how close we can get."

For the first time in however many years, I love how small this bed is. And I love how Micah knows the ways to use it to his advantage. Every night and day with him is brighter than the previous. Every one a new experience.

And I never want them to end.

NINETEEN

MICAH

WEEKENDS AT ROAR don't hold the same level of energy and exhilaration since Peyton switched days.

Yes, the club is packed with bustling bodies. Loud music spills from the speakers and the air reeks of sweat and hops. Flashes of blue and yellow and red lights hit gyrating bodies and casual bystanders. Everything *looks* the same as it always has.

The missing factor, though, is Peyton. Her heart-stopping smile and infectious laughter. How people hung out at the bar more often because she chatted with them. Funny to say, but I also miss watching her flirt with customers.

Yeah, I have that level of confidence in Peyton and our relationship. Her flirtatious nature exists only between us and with the customers inside these walls. With the customers, it is more about retention and tips. She may not collect tips anymore, but she wants the other staff members to get paid well too.

I finish pouring a round of beers, then tell Caleb I will be back after rounds. He, Adam, and Kaylynn handle the bar while Charity and Jake bus and serve tables. I check in with both of them first. Ask if either need help or if they've had any customer issues.

Then I weave my way toward the front to check in with Ted and Julio. Ask about current occupancy and if there is anything I need to know about. Thankfully, we don't get too many people who cause a ruckus. The occasional belligerent person goes berserk and tries to cause problems. But our team is a solid unit and we don't put up with shit.

"Let me know if anything comes up," I tell them and wander the club's perimeter.

A few weeks back, Sean and Ani invested in wireless communication for the busier nights. Walkies with wired earpieces. Makes me feel like a sleuth or retail security guard. On countless occasions, I respond with "over and out" or "roger that." At this point, it is a running joke to see how goofy we all act over the walkies.

I spend the next ten minutes against the wall opposite the bar. Mindlessly scrolling through social media, I look up every now and then to check the crowd. Bored with my phone, I pocket it and wind my way toward the office. Saturday is one of two days Roar only has one manager on staff. The other night being Monday, when Peyton manages Charity Bingo night solo.

Feet from the office door, I jolt as my walkie crackles in my ear. "Hey, Micah?" Caleb speaks a little too loudly into the mic. Probably to be heard over the music.

I press the button on the corded earpiece. "What's up, Caleb?"

"There's a woman at the bar asking for you."

The first person I picture is Peyton, but I dismiss the idea as quick as it appears. One, she wouldn't come here on her night off unless something was going on. Not only that, but Caleb would refer to Peyton by name. And why would she come to the bar for me. Simple; she wouldn't. Peyton would have texted or come in through the back. She has the means to find me without asking Caleb.

The next person that comes to mind is Janine. Which freaks me the fuck out. There would be no reason for Janine to come into Roar, much less ask for me. Everything with her and the whole pregnancy situation got resolved a week and a half ago. No valid reason would bring Janine here. I expect to never see or hear from her again.

So, who the hell is here? What woman would come here asking for me?

A shiver rolls up my spine at the idea of some other woman claiming some other bullshit.

Nope. Not happening, universe. No more bullshit. You hear me?

"Did she give her name?" I ask, undecided if I want to peer around the end of the hall and look.

"No. When I offered to get you, she paled."

How fucking weird. A woman comes to the bar and specifically asks for me. But when Caleb says he will get me, she freaks. Why? What purpose does that serve?

"Is she still at the bar?" I walk closer to the open end of the hall and stop a foot short.

"No." He pauses, but still has the button pressed. "She's walking toward the door. White dress, brown hair."

From the end of the hall, I scan the crowd between the bar and door, looking for said woman. When I spy the head of brown hair and white dress, my blood turns to lava.

"What the fuck?" I whisper-growl to myself.

Weaving through the crowd is a brunette with a frame I will never forget. Not because she is drop-dead gorgeous. But because the last time I saw her, she was stark naked, riding another man's cock. One never forgets a moment like that.

Rochelle fucking Cook.

The simple fact she stepped foot in Roar has me nauseous. More than a year has passed since I caught her cheating—moaning another man's name in my bed without care—and ended our relationship. Needless to say, I replaced the bed the next day. No way in hell was I touching or sleeping in a bed someone else fucked my supposed girlfriend in.

My entire relationship with Rochelle wasn't bad. The beginning was absolute fire. We laughed and enjoyed each other's company. Went places and had fun together. But… each month of the twelve we were together became less fire and more monotonous. I didn't see it at first; blinded by infatuation and what I thought was love. Once the relationship ended, I saw everything with new perspective.

And through the grapevine, I learned Rochelle had been unfaithful more than once. Each occurrence was a knife to the chest. Hence, my unwillingness to invest myself with anyone else.

Until Peyton.

Peyton is the light I need in life. Sunshine on the darkest, shittiest day. She gives me hope and promise for the life I never knew I wanted until her. Not necessarily picket fences and immaculate gardens and two-point-five kids. But a life filled with laughter and joy, wonder and intimacy. A life of adventure and challenge and thousands of memories.

"Thanks, Caleb. If you need anything else, I'll be in the office."

"Everything alright?"

I turn on my heel and stroll down the hall and into the office. Closing the door, I flip the lock into place. "Yep. All good." Peachy fucking keen.

Micah: Be there in ten.
Peyton: Perfect timing. Pizza just arrived.

On more than one occasion, the word *love* has come to mind when talking with or thinking of Peyton. Oddly enough, it doesn't freak me out. Not like it did past me and guys in my inner circle.

Love is an anomaly. Every life form on the planet experiences love in some capacity. For a parent, friend, family member, or partner. Each type different from the previous. But one difference happens among humans versus all others.

Humans often resist what they feel. Especially when it comes to love. Time and again, they fear voicing emotion for someone. Fear the outcome it may bring. The possibility of rejection weighs heavier than acceptance.

Why?

When did humans start to fear the key to our existence? When did loving someone become something to dread? Wish I had the answers. Right now—as my heart pounds a vicious rhythm and dizziness whirls beneath my diaphragm—answers would be handy.

I park my truck across and a few spaces over from Peyton. Cutting the engine, I stare a moment at her bedroom window. Watch her silhouette haloed by the soft lamplight in her room. Her form, her profile, soft and angelic. Watch as she combs her fingers through her hair and secures it with a hair tie. The move makes me want to run my fingers through her silky, wavy locks.

The times I have been on the cusp of dropping the infamous *L* word, I force myself to resist.

I resist because I don't know if Peyton is ready to hear

the word. I resist because I don't want to ruin what we have if my emotional decree isn't reciprocated. Granted, my worries may be all for nothing. But no use in voicing how I feel until the time is right.

And the time hasn't arrived. Not yet.

Exiting the truck, I grab my overnight bag and stroll across the lot to her door. Seconds after I knock, the door swings open and her bright smile greets me. Renders me speechless, breathless. Has me swallowing past the knot in my throat as my heart rattles in my rib cage.

And just like that, all coherent thought goes out the window. That four-letter word scoots a little closer to the tip of my tongue.

"Hey," I croak out, then swallow. Stepping into her, I tug at the hem of her shirt, bring her closer and press my lips to hers. "You look cute." I skim the side of her nose with the tip of mine.

"Cute, huh?" Peyton glances down at the oversized band tee and baggy sweats. *My band tee and sweats*. Fuck, I love her in my clothes. "Do I get to say you look cute when you wear them?"

I tip my head back and laugh. "Sure. If it makes you happy, I don't give a fuck." Then I pull her in, kiss her harder, and close the door behind me.

The night goes much the same as normal. We eat dinner, snuggle on the couch watching an episode of her show choice or mine, then we fall into bed but don't sleep for hours. Everything else in the world slips away.

And that four-letter word begs to be spoken as she

wraps her limbs around me and falls into a deep sleep. This right here... life couldn't be more perfect.

TWENTY

PEYTON

Rolling over, cool sheets greet me along with the morning sun brightening my lids. With a groan, I pat the bed in search of Micah's warm body and come up empty. Slowly peeling my eyes open, the room comes into focus.

Why are the blinds not shut all the way? I never forget to crank them closed before bed. But I answer my own question as flashes of Micah's lips and hands and weight on me replay in my memory. His body hovering as he slowly moved in and out of me, eyes always connected.

As of recent, sex with Micah has been different. Better. More... just more.

Some nights feel like a fight to the death. Me ripping off his clothes, or vice versa. Lips smashed together and tongues at war as we try to fulfill our hunger, our insatiable *need* for one another. Growls and screams of pain and pleasure and everything in between.

But... there are also nights filled with tenderness.

A subtle touch of fingertips. Kisses so soft, I question whether his lips met my lips or skin at all. I know they did, though. The prickling tingle they leave in their wake grows, grows, grows until heat licks my skin from the inside out. Spreads slow and steady until it consumes every inch and I combust internally. Our bodies rock and glide in sync without hurry. Unearth a bond, a force we never knew existed but can't live without.

Now that I have Micah in my life, I don't picture a day without him. Nor do I plan to.

Laughter echoes down the hall and through my door. Laughter from the man missing from my bed. And laughter from the man who sleeps across the hall.

I toss the covers aside and slip on the sweats and shirt I wore last night. Combing fingers through my tangled hair, I pull it back, twist and secure it with a hair tie. After a quick trip to the bathroom to freshen up, I wander down the hall as quietly as possible. Tiptoe to the edge and hope neither of them spot me right away.

Peering around the corner, I catch sight of Micah and Reese. Both in the kitchen, backs to me, and cooking. Not sure who cooks what, but the scent of biscuits, peppers and onions, bacon, and eggs hits me with the first full breath I take.

My stomach rumbles so loud, I am surprised neither of them hear. I press the heel of my hand to my stomach. *Just another minute.*

Micah and Reese carry on a conversation as they cook breakfast. They speak loud enough for me to hear their voices, but soft enough the words are gibberish. No doubt, I have been the subject of their conversation at some point, if not now. And that is okay.

Seeing them like this—talking like old friends, sharing a laugh, existing in the same space—creates this ever-expanding warmth beneath my breastbone. A merriment of my past and future—not that I am getting ahead of myself. I do see Micah in my future for years to come, though.

Unable to deal with my stomach trying to eat itself any longer, I step into the open living space that connects with the dining area and kitchen. Neither Micah nor Reese hear me, so I sit at the breakfast bar until one does.

"You seriously can't cook anything other than breakfast?" Reese asks Micah.

"Don't judge me," Micah retorts on a laugh. "Mom tried. Just didn't stick."

"Trust me, you want to learn." As the words roll off his tongue, Reese reaches for his coffee and spots me. "Morning, sunshine. How long you been eavesdropping?"

Micah peeks over his shoulder and gifts me with my favorite smile of his. He doesn't care if I heard every word.

I stick my tongue out at Reese. "Only long enough for you to learn Micah can't cook. He does make kick-ass breakfasts, though."

"Thanks, hellcat." He winks.

Jutting my chin toward the stove. "Speaking of breakfast. What're we having?"

"Southwest omelets, bacon, and biscuits," Micah answers.

Before I voice my opinion, my stomach groans and responds loud enough both guys laugh. "Shut up." I flip them both the middle finger. "Is it almost ready? I need to get dressed soon."

As if they have worked in kitchens together their entire life, they plate up my food. Micah places the omelet on the plate, then Reese adds three strips of bacon and a biscuit. Micah sets the plate in front of me and hands me a fork. Reese fetches the butter and honey while Micah pops a mug under the Keurig drip and presses the large button.

If they aren't careful, a girl could get used to this. Two guys tending to her. But I keep the thought to myself.

One—Reese and I will only ever be friends. I know that. He knows that. But Micah may still misconstrue the statement if said aloud.

Two—I honestly don't think I would ever be able to mentally handle more than one person in my life. My romantic life, that is. If I were into one-night stands or casual, no-strings-attached relationships, I might consider the idea. But I'm not. So, the point is moot.

Halfway through my breakfast, Micah plops down beside me and starts eating his own. Considering I eat slower than the average person, we will probably finish at the same time. Mine and Micah's plates are almost empty when Reese sits on the third stool.

"You seeing Ms. J today?" Reese asks around a mouthful of omelet.

"Yeah." My fork clatters against my plate. "I hate not being there as often. Seeing her every other Sunday feels wrong. Like I've abandoned her." I pick at my biscuit and eat it bit by bit. "Hope she's better today."

"Me too, sunshine." He swallows his bite. "Having lunch with Aunt Leanne after?"

"Yes." Spending time with Aunt Leanne is one of the week's highlights. "She wants to take me to some new deli. If she says it's good, I'll love it."

Micah bumps my knee with his. "Busy day."

"I love it, though." Busy doesn't cover it, but I love seeing people who make me happy. Hopefully, I will add Micah's family to the list when we have dinner with them tonight.

When I clear my plate, Micah takes both ours to the sink, rinses them off, and places them in the dishwasher.

"He's domesticated," Reese announces with a shit-eating grin. "Does he have a clone?"

I chuckle and scoot off my stool. "Just a sister. But I don't think she's looking for love."

"Boo. Well, let me know if you find his doppelgänger in the world."

"What happened to Trent?" Last I knew, he and his beau were still together. Which is a record for Reese. Long-term relationships aren't high priority for him—not that I judge how he lives his life.

Reese drops his head between his shoulders. "He

wanted to take a break while on his work trip. Said he didn't want me to feel tied down." Reese lifts his head and meets my gaze. "But I like it when he ties me down."

"I almost felt bad for you," I say as I slap his arm. "Ass."

"No, seriously. I like him. Enough to make roots. But that's a story for another day and when he returns." Reese slaps my ass. "Now, go get ready for Ms. J. I want my crochet beanie before winter."

In the bathroom, I crank the shower and strip out of my clothes. As the sweats slide down my thighs, Micah steps up behind me, grabs my hips, and peppers kisses along my shoulder.

"Don't have much time," I moan out as he nips the skin below my ear.

"A quickie." *Kiss. Lick. Suck.* "Then I'll wash you."

Will I learn how to say no to this man again? Don't see it happening. And the notion doesn't bother me one bit.

Ms. Jenkins has lost weight. A lot of weight. And her skin doesn't seem to bolster the same radiance I usually see. It appears more translucent and wilted. Will she crumble if I touch her?

Seeing her like this—slowly fading—stirs up

unpleasant memories. Memories that brought me to work at Gulfside in the first place.

Naturally, death is a part of life. Is unavoidable and happens to every species. Doesn't mean I have to like it. Doesn't mean I need to be okay accepting it.

"How've you been? Feel like I never see you anymore."

Ms. Jenkins stares at the crochet hook and yarn in my hands. "Your cap looks great. Who's the lucky recipient?"

Why didn't she answer my question? She never avoids answers. In fact, she usually tells me what is on her mind without hesitation. Gives me her two cents and a few quarters to boot.

So, why the evasion now?

I set down the beanie project in my lap and lay a hand on hers. Her hand is so cold. Too cold. And her skin feels as if it could peel away any minute. The need to wrap her in a thick blanket and hug her close overwhelms me imme-diately. Something about this entire situation is off and I don't like her obvious avoidance.

"Tell me what's wrong. Please," I say an octave above a whisper.

Ms. Jenkins sets down her own project—a baby blanket—and faces me as best she can. "You're such a sweet girl, Peyton." A cool hand cups my cheek as she gives me a soft smile. "I'm just an old lady. And my time is almost up. That's how life works."

For a minute, I stare into her warm brown eyes and digest what she said. Yes, eighty-seven is old. But I have known several people to live well into their nineties. Does she think she won't? Why would she think that?

"Last I saw you, everything seemed good. What's changed?"

Her thumb brushes slowly over my cheekbone. "Not sure. I just feel a change inside me. It isn't painful. More like my body is preparing for the inevitable."

A tear rolls down my cheek. "I don't want you to go."

The corner of her mouth lifts as she wipes away the tear. "I know. But when it's time, it's time. We can't fight what is meant to be. But we can use what time we have left wisely. Pass on pieces of ourselves so we live on in others." She looks down at the crocheted beanie in my lap. "Life has more meaning when we share and enjoy it with someone. That is my wish for you."

"Your wish?"

"Yes, sweet Peyton. Live your life. Seek adventure. Learn new things. Don't live your life in fear. Share yourself with others, so you too can live on through them when your time comes."

I don't want to leave here today. Ms. Jenkins says to live without fear. But how can I do that when I fear what will happen when I walk out the front door today? Why does today feel like *goodbye* and not *see you next time*?

"Why are you saying all this?" I ask through fresh tears.

She lifts her other hand to frame my face. "You know why."

"What if I want to be selfish and keep you?"

Her thumbs wipe at my tears. "As much as you want to, you won't be. It's my time. And Stephen is waiting for me. I won't be alone."

Oh god. Right here, in the middle of the community room at Gulfside, I am about to lose my shit. Weep and wail like a child. Throw a fit because this isn't fair. Life isn't fair.

And yes, it is petty of me to want her to stay when she seems ready to go. But I am so tired of loss. Downright exhausted at feeling it time and time again. Ms. Jenkins may not be my family by blood, but she is my family nonetheless. Not seeing and hugging and chatting with her will rip me apart. Not hearing her stories or crocheting beanies or sitting in the sun with her will gut me.

She drops her hands from my cheeks after one last swipe at my tears. "I have lived a long, happy, and fulfilling life, Peyton. Today will be the last day you cry about me. Understood?"

"How can you ask that of me?"

"How can I not?" She tucks loose strands behind my ear. "Last thing I want is people mopey. Remember all the wonderful moments. The ones that make you smile and laugh. Those are the ones that matter most. Not some morbid ritual where people think only of loss and not all the joy that person brought to others. Remember the joy, Peyton. Then go out and live your life. Experience love and the world. Hopefully, both at the same time. And when you remember me, I want you to think about our talks and crocheting and strolls outside. You hear me?"

I nod and wipe under each eye. "Yes, ma'am."

"Now, let's finish this cap and blanket."

The rest of my time at Gulfside is spent learning all the final touches on my project as well as hers. And when I walk out the front door, I do so with a heavy, full heart. I pray today isn't the last time I see Ms. Jenkins, but know the possibility is there. Not that I will ever be okay with losing someone I care about, but at least we had today. At least, I got to say goodbye.

"So, you're meeting the parents tonight, huh?" Aunt Leanne asks before she shoves the club sandwich between her lips.

"Yeah. From what Micah's said, they sound like nice people."

"Then why do you look nauseous?"

Because I am. Because today has a lot happening and my body is on the fritz with how to handle it all.

"Ms. Jenkins pretty much told me she's dying today." It isn't the sole reason for why I feel—and probably look —like garbage. But it is a major player in the game.

Aunt Leanne sets down her sandwich. "Oh, Peyton. I'm so sorry." She moves to my side of the table and hugs me a moment before returning to her seat. "Do you think she meant it? Or is she just losing it?"

This crossed my mind more than once as I finished my shift at Gulfside. The possibility something triggered her to say what she said. A friend in the facility passing. A family member passing. Death changes people's perspectives. It has certainly changed mine.

"Don't know. Part of me *feels* she won't be there in two weeks. But I pray she is." I sip my drink and the cool liquid does nothing to settle the unease in my chest. "She said some pretty profound things today. Things people say when they aren't sure another chance will happen."

Aunt Leanne reaches across the table and takes my hand. "I'm glad you had today with her."

"Me too."

She gives my hand a gentle squeeze, then releases it. "Now, what can I do to make tonight less stressful?"

I shake my head and laugh. "Wish I knew. Not like I've never met the parents in previous relationships."

"So, why the jitters?"

The answer crawls its way to the tip of my tongue. Ready to escape, but I restrain it a little longer. Right here, right now, with Aunt Leanne, isn't the time to confess.

"Because everything is different with Micah." And that little fact excites and frightens me equally.

TWENTY-ONE

MICAH

Lifting a hand, I knock on Peyton's front door.

On the other side, a thump sounds. Followed by Peyton saying "shit" and Reese laughing at whatever happened. The lock disengages a second before the door flies open.

"Hi," Peyton huffs out. "I'm not ready."

I step in and shut the door. "No worries, I'm early." I check her head to toe and bite back laughter. "You okay?"

Reese laughs again and Peyton rolls her eyes. "Fine. Just bumped the wall trying to put my shoe on."

Peyton wanders down the hall to her room and I follow in her wake. Inside, I close the door and sit on the bed. For a moment, I track her rapid-fire movement as she plucks clothes from the closet and dresser, then stuffs them in the bag she brings to the house.

Tonight, she put on a golden maxi dress and black flats that peek out when she walks. Her hair is down in thick, soft waves and stops an inch or two below her mid-back. A light layer of gloss makes her lips shimmer. And with each pass in front of me, I inhale my favorite scent—Peyton's coconut mint.

She stops within reach and looks around the room. "Got that and that," she mumbles to herself. She carries on, ticking things off on her fingers.

I lift my hands and grab her hips. "Hey," I say and tip my head back to see her better. She stops and meets my gaze. "Something wrong?"

"No. Just making sure I have everything. I think I have everything. What if I forget something?" The words spill from her lips faster than her movement around the room.

I rise from the bed and pull her into me. Releasing a hip, I bring the hand to her cheek and caress it with my thumb. "Are you nervous about tonight? About meeting my parents?" Her eyes widen just enough for me to know the answer is yes. "You have nothing to worry about. Mom can be a little much at times, but Dad levels her out. Plus, if she says anything *I* don't find appropriate, I'll open my mouth. She gets excited."

"What if they don't like me?"

What a ridiculous question. Who would not like Peyton? Petty bitches of the past, but no one else.

"What if they love you?" I counter, biting my tongue so I don't add *"like I do."*

She huffs and a few strands close to her lips fly up and tickle my face. But I don't brush them away. Instead, I relish all the contacts and connections we share. Leaning in, I press a chaste kiss to her lips and come away with glossy coconut on mine.

"C'mon. If you forgot anything, we'll figure it out." I take her hand in mine and weave our fingers together. With my free hand, I shoulder her overnight bag. "Ready?"

After a deep breath, she nods. "Yeah. Let me grab my purse."

We say good night to Reese, hop in the truck and toss her bag in the back cab seating. Peyton picks a music playlist from my phone as I steer us onto the highway. The drive is spent with our fingers weaving in and out of each other's and rock music quietly vibrating from the speakers.

Less than thirty minutes later, I park next to Shelly's Beetle in Mom and Dad's driveway. Surprisingly, Shelly isn't in her car waiting like prior dinner nights. Maybe —hopefully—she tames Mom a bit before we step inside.

Inhaling deeply, I open my door then walk around to open Peyton's. With her hand in mine, we stroll to the front door in silence. Peyton may be nervous to meet my parents, but I am nervous too. I am nervous Mom may be too eccentric or Dad too dull. Shelly may be a little extra tonight, too, but I doubt it.

After Mom's declaration of wanting us to find happiness with another person, Shelly and I remain tight lipped when possible. Arranged marriages aren't really a thing around here anymore, but I wouldn't put it past Mom to try.

"Ready?" I ask as my hand hovers over the knob.

Peyton nods. "Ready as I'll ever be."

I twist the knob and the door flies open with Shelly on the other side. "You guys making out?"

Please don't let this be a precursor for the entire evening. "No, Shelly, we were not making out. This isn't high school. I act like an adult when necessary."

"Whatever." She rolls her eyes at me, then gives Peyton a big smile and hug. "Glad you're here. Maybe Mom will be less... maybe she'll just be less."

Peyton's eyes widen as she death grips my hand. I stroke the top of her hand with my thumb in reassurance. "It'll be fine. Quit freaking her out, Shell."

"Sorry," she says with a wince.

Inside the house, we follow Shelly toward the kitchen. Hints of garlic and cheese and bread float in the air. Mom asked if Peyton had food allergies, but didn't tell me what was on the menu tonight. By the smell, I'd guess lasagna. Guess we will find out soon enough.

We round the corner and Mom stops whatever conversation she and Dad are having. She looks from me to Peyton, to our hands and back up to me. The warmest, gentlest smile lights her face as she walks toward us.

"Hey, honey. Glad you made it." She gives me a longer than normal hug. "And you must be Peyton," she says. "I'm Nicole. It's wonderful to meet you." Without permission, Mom hugs Peyton.

I stare at the embrace with shock and embarrassment heating my cheeks. Mom *never* hugs strangers. Ever. Peyton and I are in a relationship, but she has never hugged any of my past girlfriends the first time they met.

"Mom, let's not scare her. Okay?"

Mom detaches her octopus tentacles from Peyton and takes a step back. "Oh, I'm sorry, dear. Don't know what came over me."

The oven timer goes off and rescues us from another round of awkwardness. "Be back in a minute," I announce. "I'm going to show Peyton around the house."

"Dinner will be on the table in a couple minutes," Mom replies.

Hand in hand, I lead Peyton through the house and away from my overzealous mother. I point and prattle off each room. "Dining and living room. Mom's home office, formerly Shelly's bedroom. Dad's home office, formerly my bedroom. Bathroom. Parents' bedroom." Then I lead her into the last room on the right and close the door. "Guest room."

The room is minimal, with white walls and smoky blue accents. A queen bed with gray-blue bedding, a white bed frame, and a mountain of throw pillows. A small, four-drawer white dresser and matching bedside table. Gray-blue curtains against white wooden blinds. The white-framed pictures on the wall of blue marine life or beachy images.

Not sure how my mother managed to replicate the same color for the entire room, but she did. On occasion, I wonder if she hired someone and gave them a color swatch. Wouldn't surprise me.

"Doing okay?" I ask as I step into Peyton and hug her close. "Mom has been a little much recently. Not sure what provoked the change, but I hope it fades. Soon."

Light laughter spills from her lips. "It's fine. All mothers probably go through this stage. Wanting to see their children happy as adults." Peyton breaks the hug, walks around the room and stops in front of one of the frames. "I won't try to guess how my mom will be when you meet her. Generally, she's pretty laid back. But I've also seen her at her best and worst."

I step up behind her and wrap my arms around her front. "If she asks weird questions, you don't have to answer. Shell and I are used to deflecting when necessary. You can use a code word, if she makes you uncomfortable." I chuckle but mean every word. Mom isn't *bad*, she just gets intense. Especially if you don't know her.

Peyton rests her hands over mine. "It'll be fine. No matter who we are, parents are always strange to us or people close to us."

"Still think you should have a code word," I mumble into her hair.

"Fine," she says with a laugh. "How about sushi?"

"Sushi?"

"Mmhm."

"How the hell would you work that into conversation?"

She shrugs. "Maybe I won't have to. But if I do, I'll figure it out."

"Alright, sushi. Let's go before they think we're fucking on the bed."

"What?" Peyton's face pales as her eyes go wide.

"Joking, hellcat. C'mon."

We join everyone in the dining room and sit at the table. Each place setting has a small salad and dipping oil for bread. Bread baskets sit at either end of the table—because we love bread. Mom brings out a large casserole dish and sets it at the heart of the table.

"Baked ziti, made with creamy pesto instead of marinara," she announces with a glowing smile.

Peyton shifts in her seat and stares at me with a slack jaw. "Your mom makes dishes like this and all you can cook is breakfast?"

Across from us, Shelly snort-laughs and tries to cover it with a cough.

"Shut it, Shell."

Mom joins in on Shelly's laughter for a second, then stops when she sees my face. "Sorry, Micah. It is funny." Mom shifts her gaze to Peyton. "I've tried to teach Micah for years and it doesn't stick. But I refuse to give up. One day, he'll surprise me, or you, and make something else."

Once all the food is on the table, everyone settles and starts on their salad. Easy conversation flows around the table. Thankfully, Mom hasn't said anything off-putting the entire time.

Every time she glances over to Peyton's and my side of

the table, though, I see the sparkle in her eye. The barely noticeable uptick at the corners of her mouth and eyes. And when Peyton speaks, Mom listens. She lets her say every word, then comments back as if she and Peyton have chatted hundreds of times.

By the end of the evening, we leave with full bellies, a heaping container of leftovers, and warm hugs.

"That wasn't so bad," I say once we are on the road.

"Your mom is nice. She loves you both and just wants the best for you and Shelly."

"Yeah, she does. Glad she didn't make you uncomfortable." I lace my fingers with hers, lift them to my lips, and kiss her knuckles.

A couple songs and commercials on the radio later, I park in the driveway and we walk into the house. I lock the dead bolt and drop her overnight bag to the floor. She opens her mouth to ask something, but I cut her off with my lips to hers.

I frame her face in my hands and kiss the hell out of her. Her hands snake around my waist and fist the back hem of my jeans. We stumble toward the bedroom, our lips never apart. When her legs bump the mattress, I kiss along her jaw, down her neck, along her shoulder.

Grabbing the back collar of my shirt, I yank it off and toss it on the floor. I reach out, trace my fingertips along the dress seam at her breasts. Her eyes drift shut as a shiver rolls through her body.

But I don't want her to shut out the world. Not tonight. Not now.

I trail my fingers up the column of her throat to her chin and tip it up slightly. "Open your eyes, Peyton." Violet irises meet my blues and hum with anticipation. The gray flecks sparkle with delight. I lean in, my lips a whisper over hers as I hold her gaze. "I love you, Peyton."

The sentiment flows with such ease. My whole body comes alive. A blazing buzz spreads like an electrical current, zapping and sparking and jolting anew. Breath fills me with life as my heart learns a new rhythm.

"I love you, too." Peyton closes the space between us and kisses me as if we have found ourselves. Here, in this moment. Together.

We peel away our clothes and rediscover each other. Learn who we are with our proclamations in the open. Make love to each other until we are bone tired and in a pile of tangled limbs. And in the early morning hours, I hug her close to my side and whisper I love you in her ear as we drift off to sleep.

Happy, sated, and head over heels in love.

TWENTY-TWO

PEYTON

"Stop!" I shout between giggles.

"Stop what?" Micah digs his fingertips into the side of my rib cage for the umpteenth time.

"Tickling me." I pry at his fingers in the hopes of getting free. But he has a death grip on my waist. "We need…" *Tickle.* "To get ready…" *Tickle.* "For work." *Laugh.* "Oh, god." I clamp my thighs together and clench my internal muscles. "Seriously, Micah. Stop. I'm going to pee."

He digs in harder and laughs. "Liar."

"No, seriously." If I don't make it to the bathroom now, this won't be pretty. I tug him in that direction and hope he picks up on how severe the situation is. "My bladder is about to let go."

He drops his hands. *Thank fuck.* I bolt to the toilet, drop my pants and call it a win that I made it in time.

Micah walks in and winces as I finish up. "Sorry.

Didn't mean for that to happen."

"Yeah, yeah. But remember this…" I point a finger at him. "If I say I have to pee, I'm not joking." I stare at his pouty lip while I wash up. For a split second, I consider apologizing. But I let it go.

"Sorry, hellcat." He pulls me in for a hug. I hesitate on returning the hug, wondering if he will tickle me again. When he doesn't, I wrap my arms around his middle and lean into him.

Cool air hits my skin as he brushes hair off my shoulder. Before a shiver passes, warm lips kiss the width of my shoulder, along the curve of my neck and up to that spot beneath my ear. Hands roam the landscape of my body — gentle and rough, caressing and kneading.

One hand slides up my spine, dives into my hair, fists the locks and tugs back. The brightest constellation stares down at me and I lick my lips. Clench my thighs for a different reason.

Micah reads me like an open book. Sees the need in my eyes. Feels my taut nipples on his chest and subtle grind of my hips.

He lowers his lips, stopping a breath above mine. "We don't have time," he says with a smirk on his lips.

"Please," I moan. At this rate, I am willing to be late or speed to work, if necessary. Not like we aren't always early.

Micah tightens his grip on my hair and licks the seam of my lips. "Gonna be quick and dirty. You good with that?"

"You know I am."

Then, he releases my hair, spins me around to face the bed, yanks my pants and underwear down, and forces me to bend at the waist. With a clunk, his pants and briefs hit the floor. He draws circles on my skin just above my ass crack.

As I open my mouth to tell him to quit teasing me, his finger glides between my cheeks. He pauses at the tight hole and presses slightly. "One day, I'll claim this too." The rumble in his tone and the promise in his words make me push into his touch. "Not now, hellcat," he growls out. "But soon."

His finger slips lower, separates my lips and toys with my clit. I fist the comforter and grind against his touch.

"So wet and eager." *Whack*. His free hand slaps my ass. "I love when you're starved for me."

His finger vanishes, but is quickly replaced with the tip of his cock. He rubs the head between my lips—up and down, over and over. Teasing and taunting.

Then he slams forward and fills me. "Jesus fuck," I belt out as I claw the bedding.

"Hold on, hellcat. Quick and dirty time."

Micah slides a hand up my spine, circles around the front of my throat, and tightens his grip. With the other hand on my hip, he holds me in place as his cock pistons between my thighs. Balls slapping my clit. My moans and his bouncing off the walls while pheromones and arousal fog the air.

When the pitch of my cries escalates, he shifts the

hand on my hip to my nipple and tweaks the tight bud. His hand around my throat constricts and I go into sensation overload. Heat spirals up my spine, spreads across my chest and up my neck as my walls tighten around his cock. He twists my nipple harder. Slams into me with more aggression. Tips me over the edge and jumps after me.

"God, I love when you come," he growls in my ear and releases my neck. "Fucking spectacular."

"Thanks," I say on a laugh. "I'll take it as a compliment."

We walk in the back of Roar—still early—with loony smiles on our faces. Good thing the staff doesn't arrive when we do. It would be ridiculously difficult to hide our euphoria.

Micah and I decide to split tasks to make the evening easier. He will set up for Karaoke Night while I work on scheduling and payroll. Recently, we started dealing with invoices and ordering on Tuesdays and Fridays. Days when we don't work together, but still have another manager on duty. It frees up our joint work nights more and gets us off the floor most of the night when everyone else has it handled.

It isn't long before the staff arrives and Roar opens. The bar lines with patrons ordering drinks. A line forms near the makeshift stage as people add their name to the karaoke roster. Tables fill with people and conversations. And it isn't long before the first singer steps on stage and blesses us with their song selection and voice.

Pouring a beer from the tap, I look up and spot the group walking in. I finish pouring and serve the customer before pressing the button on my headset.

"Starlight."

"Hellcat."

"Everyone's here."

"Be out in a sec." As the walkie cuts out, Micah rounds the corner with bottles from the storage room in his hands.

We both help with drink orders until the line is manageable for Mable and Josiah. Then we exit the bar alley and join our friends at the table.

Great songs spill from the speakers as squawky voices belt out lyrics. Our friends drink beer and discuss which songs they will sing when their turn comes. Micah and I sit back, join in the conversation, laugh and enjoy the evening and our surroundings.

Shelly tugs Cora toward the stage as both my and Micah's walkies crackle in our ears. "Boss man," Ted calls out. "Someone I admitted in asked if you're working tonight."

I meet Micah's gaze with a scrunched brow. He shrugs. "Did you catch their name?"

"No, sorry. But she's wearing a red dress and has brown hair."

Closing my eyes, I take a deep breath and search for

my inner zen. Never would I suspect Micah of adultery. So, my mind doesn't go in that direction when I hear a woman is asking for him. Instead, my mind travels to the long list of women he was with over the years and prays another one isn't coming at him with some outlandish accusation.

Micah spins to face me head-on. "Please don't freak out."

"Not the best way to start a conversation," I say.

He nods. "Saturday, I was headed to the office after rounds to catch up on paperwork. Caleb informed me over the walkie that a woman asked for me. By the time he brought it up, she was headed for the exit. I only caught the back of her, but knew who it was."

"Who?"

An angry nest of hornets buzzes in my belly and sends venom through my veins. I am sick and tired of all these women. Do they not understand the concept of one-night stands? From what Micah told me, he made it abundantly clear to all of them.

"Rochelle," he says, loud enough for only me to hear.

Rochelle? As in his ex-girlfriend? As in the woman who fucked another man in his bed and crushed his heart? If Rochelle is here, this isn't some pregnancy situation. This is next level. And I have had it with the bullshit.

I lock eyes with Micah. See fear as his eyes dart between mine and sweat slicks his brow. Feel anxiety roll off him as he clenches my hands and waits for me to say something. Anything.

"Ted?"

"Yes, Miss Peyton?"

"Please be on standby to escort someone from the premises."

Micah's eyes widen. "What're you doing?"

"Handling this; after we figure out what she wants."

Out of nowhere, Shelly stops singing mid-song. Cora slaps Shelly's arm. "Too drunk to sing already?" Cora teases. But when I look to Shelly, her eyes are laser-focused behind me.

One-way ticket to party town coming up.

"There you are," a brunette says as she stops in front of Micah, in front of us.

Dressed in an overpriced dress and heels, Rochelle has the audacity to rest her hand on Micah's shoulder as she steps into his space. Micah shirks from her touch and inches back.

"First, don't touch me. Second, what are you doing here, Rochelle?"

The woman smiles as if Micah didn't just say to back the fuck up nicely. I ball my fingers into fists and keep them pinned at my sides. I will let Micah be the nice one. But if this bitch doesn't catch on soon...

"Wanted to see you. I miss you."

"Are you fucking kidding me right now?" Micah says louder than before, and eyes dart our way. "You miss me? What, did your fuckboy leave you?"

Rochelle jerks her head back as if slapped. "No need to be ugly. To answer your question, no, he didn't break up with me. I broke it off with him. He was too immature. And like I said, I miss you."

She reaches forward and is inches from touching Micah when I rise from my stool. "Do not touch him."

"Who are you?" she asks with a snarl. "His flavor of the day?"

I step closer, invading her space, and use the few inches I have on her to get in her face. She doesn't back down but looks a little gray in the face. For a moment, I don't say anything. I simply stare down at her. When she swallows, I know I have her.

"Actually, it doesn't matter who I am. What matters is he isn't yours. Hasn't been for quite some time. You don't deserve him. Hell, you don't deserve anyone."

"You don't know me," she bites back. "How dare you—"

"How dare I what? Not be a frigid bitch. Not treat someone like trash." I hold my hands in front of me, palms up, and wave my fingers. "Let's hear it. And it better be good." Rochelle looks past me to Micah. "No." I push her back. "You don't get to look at him."

"I don't know who you think you are, but if you touch me again, I'll call the police."

I tip my head back and laugh. "And I'll laugh as they issue you a trespassing notice because you're harassing an employee." I force her back as I step farther into her. "You can go peacefully or not. The choice is yours."

"You don't know who you're messing with," she bites out. "He's only good for sex. So, you can have him."

A fuse lights in my veins. Burns slow and hot as the flame gets closer to the ticking bomb beneath my rib cage. My breathing kicks up a degree as my cheeks flush. And before I give serious thought to my actions, I take a step back, grab her shoulders, rear back, and drive my knee between her legs. Hard.

Rochelle crumples to the floor and wails in pain as she grabs herself. "Bitch!"

"Right back atcha," I say with a half smile, then press the button on my walkie. "Ted?"

"On my way, Miss Peyton."

No doubt Ted heard and witnessed the entire altercation. And if anyone asked who was in the wrong here, several would say I asked the woman to leave. Did I need to get physical? No, but she wasn't backing down or following Micah's or my request to leave. Her presence was—is—unwanted, and she refused to give in. If I hadn't taken it next level, she would probably continue to harass us.

Ted helps Rochelle off the floor. Soon as she is upright, she goes on a tirade. "You'll be sorry, little girl."

"Actually" —Shelly steps up to Rochelle— "no she won't. Several of us just witnessed the whole thing. You put your hands on the manager without permission. Were asked to leave by another manager and refused. Then you threatened her. She was protecting herself."

Well, damn. Shelly is a viper. Not someone you mess with or want on your bad side. Noted. The fact she stepped up—whether for Micah, me, or us both—has my spine straighter and head higher. No doubt Shelly knows Rochelle and has some inkling of what she did to Micah. She would go to bat for him any day of the week. But for her to reinforce me, that says a lot about us—me and Shelly—and the small bond forming.

Rochelle turns her pathetic eyes in my direction. "You'll get bored of him, just like I did. Then, you'll wish I relieved you of him."

I shake my head. "Love that you're telling me why you fucked around on him, yet here you are." I look her up and down. "Begging for another chance. I feel sorry for you and your pitiful life. He's moved on. Found happiness. Found someone who loves him as much as he loves her. And you lost out. If you step foot on this property or come near me or Micah again, you'll see how much of a bitch I *can* be."

Ted guides Rochelle toward the doors as the crowd claps and cheers. I don't look away until Rochelle is out the door. And for the first time in who knows how long, I breathe.

Until Micah swoops in, cups my cheeks, and kisses the hell out of me in front of everyone. Wolf whistles and hollers to *get a room* come at us from every direction. The kiss is far from innocent as his hands roam my body. To be honest, I don't give a fuck. Because one fact is certain in this moment.

Micah Reed belongs to me. And he sure as hell is letting everyone know I belong to him. Wouldn't want it any other way.

TWENTY-THREE

MICAH

LAUGHTER MIXES with rock music as Peyton and I sit on a lounger in Jonas and Autumn's backyard. Our typical Sunday get-together underway.

Gavin and Jonas man the grill; flipping burgers, brats, and mojo-marinated chicken quarters while chatting. Autumn, Cora, and Shelly load one of the banquet tables with buns, side salads, fruit, and condiments. Penny and Rex go back and forth over something frivolous—socks in the living room. Reznor and Tatyana watch their son, Ashton, play with Clementine and Spartan. Iliana, Trevor, and Jillian—Jonas's younger sister—sit on the lounger across from us and chat about an upcoming baseball game.

Life feels pretty fucking amazing right now.

A year ago, I would not have pictured my life like this. With Peyton at my side, holding my hand and laughing at jokes told by my closest friends. A year ago, I had no smiles to give. Felt empty inside. Did all I could to fill the void. But nothing worked.

Now, I know the reason.

Fate has never been something I put much thought in. Especially when my relationship with Rochelle ended how it did. But now I give fate some credit. Give in to the notion that two people are meant to find each other and live their best life together.

Several years ago, fate brought Peyton and I together. I wasn't ready, though. She'd had her eye on me back then, but who is to say where our relationship would have gone had we gotten together.

I look toward the grill, watch how Cora latches on to every word Gavin says with hearts in her eyes. Watch how he kisses her forehead, then whispers something in her ear and causes her cheeks to flush.

Could that have been me and Peyton? There is no definite answer. Although Gavin and Cora are madly in love, shit beyond their control tore them apart early on. Fate found a way to bring them back together. If Peyton and I had been different in high school, would we have drifted apart? Or would we still be together? If our lives were different back then, I don't think we would be who we are now. Nor would we feel the same.

And that is not something I care to dwell on. The what-ifs.

What I *do* know is that I have never been happier. And I owe it all to the hellcat at my side.

I lean in and press my lips to her temple. "I love you."

Peyton stops whatever she was saying to Shelly and faces me. "Love you, too." Then she presses her lips to mine. I break the kiss all too soon, not wanting our friends to give us shit.

Gavin and Jonas announce the meat is off the grill—which is our version of a dinner bell. Everyone evacuates their seats, grabs plates, and piles them high. Minutes later, the only sound outside is the music, occasional crunch of food, and Spartan's whimper for scraps.

Off to the side, Cora asks Shelly about work and I shift my attention.

"Is the shop staying busy? Whenever I ask Mom, she says yes. But she thinks five customers in one day is busy," Cora says with a laugh.

Shelly swallows her bite and takes a sip from her beer. "It's gotten busier in the last few months. Not sure why. We've done a little more marketing, but not much. Whatever the reason, the uptick is great."

"Mom jokingly said maybe she'll retire sooner."

Shelly pales, which I find interesting. It is no secret that Shelly will take over the florist shop when Cora's mom retires. She plans to buy the business over time and make minor changes. But I don't think the plan was for her to own the shop for three to five more years. As a planner, if something changes the overall picture, Shelly freaks out.

Shelly laughs without humor. "Hope she's joking. Not quite ready to fill her shoes yet."

Cora waves her off. "I'm sure she is. Anyway... on to

less stressful topics. Have you talked to the hottie painting the shop mural?"

"What *hottie*?" I ask, shooting daggers at my little sister.

She rolls her eyes, then stabs a chunk of potato salad and stuffs it in her mouth. It's an obvious attempt to avoid the subject, so I just sit and wait and stare like the annoying older brother I am. Until she caves. And because I know my sister well, she will cave. Soon.

"Argh!" Like clockwork. "He's just some guy painting a mural on the outside of the shop. No big deal."

"Cora seems to think it's big enough a deal to bring him up," I say.

Shelly narrows her eyes at Cora. "And we will talk about *that* later." She shifts her gaze back to me. "Seriously, though. He's just some artist Elizabeth hired. Nothing else."

I stare at my sister a moment. Try to read between the lines. Zero in on the fine details she leaves out. But for some reason, she has sealed herself off. Has put on her best poker face and enforced the most neutral body language. That alone tells me there is definitely more to this. Tells me she doesn't just look at this guy as *just some artist Elizabeth hired*. She looks at him with newly formed interest.

For now, I won't push her on it. Won't make her uncomfortable and embarrass her in front of friends. But I will get more answers. Soon.

"If you say so. Just don't let Mom find out about said

no big deal or you'll never hear the end of it."

For a beat, her body sags. The only reason I don't miss it is because I know my sister. Know that finding *the one* is a big deal to her. As an avid romance reader, she is big on the fated-lovers concept. Believes everyone will get their happily ever after.

For years, she harped on most of us about destiny and love written in the stars. Now that someone pops up on her radar, she keeps secrets. Doesn't let anyone pry as she has in the past.

Maybe I need to stop by the floral shop and buy Peyton flowers next week. Find out more about this artist.

The rest of the night flows with great conversation, an intense game of *Never Have I Ever* and belly-aching laughter. Everyone says their goodbyes and goes separate ways until next week.

After the short ride home, I park in the driveway and we walk hand in hand to the door and inside. The door clicks shut and I wrap Peyton in my arms. Kiss her as if I will never get the chance again.

"What was that for?" she asks when we come up for air.

"For everything."

"Everything?"

I nod. "For the longest time, life, and the world, was a restless night. Since you, life is colorful. More brilliant."

"Bright," she adds.

"Bright," I repeat, then kiss her. "And I can't imagine life any better. Or a love any brighter."

EPILOGUE
PEYTON

One year later

MICAH STEPS up behind me and wraps me in his arms. "Almost ready?" His starry-sky irises meet mine in the mirror and, for a moment, we breathe in sync with each other.

Although Micah and I have become practically inseparable the last year, we took things slower than most couples. With our pasts, Micah and I decided there was no need to rush things.

We spent every available minute of the day together and every night in each other's arms. Yet, we waited until two months ago to move in together. The wait had nothing to do with my rent at the apartment or that we wanted occasional solitude. More like we wanted to ease into this step. Ease into sharing space full time with a new person. Ease into cohabitation.

"Yeah. One more minute."

Micah kisses my bare shoulder. "I'll wait in the living room."

He exits and leaves me to finish getting ready. I do one last once-over to make sure nothing is out of place. After a quick swipe of gloss, I tuck the tube in my purse and join Micah in the living room.

"Ready when you are," I say and offer my elbow to him.

He takes my arm and guides us out the door and to the car. We wind our way out of the neighborhood, then Micah drives us south to an undisclosed location for dinner. He hasn't told me the reason why I needed to dress up, but I suspect it has something to do with us celebrating our "official" one-year anniversary. Yes, we casually dated for weeks leading up to August tenth, but we didn't want to label our relationship.

Then a switch flipped. Since that moment, we let the world know there is an us.

Miles of highway pass before Micah exits and drives along the city streets. I have no clue where he is taking me, but I do know we are in Tampa. Two more right turns, then a left and Micah drives the car into a parking lot. No name appears on the rustic brick building, just a logo of a setting sun.

"What is this place?" I ask, staring out the window.

"You'll see. I only know about it through connections at Roar."

I spin in my seat to face him as we pull up to a valet in

a white dress shirt, black slacks, and a black tie. "Micah, this place looks really expensive."

"If it was too much, I wouldn't have brought us." He says that, but I am not buying a word of it.

The valet opens our doors and helps us out. Micah steps around the front of the car, takes my arm, and escorts me inside. The moment we step through the double oak doors, I stop breathing.

This place is expensive. Ridiculously expensive.

My heels clack on antique hardwood as we walk down a long corridor. The interior walls the same brick as the exterior. Soft white light glows from candelabra chandeliers above. Photographs from different eras sit in thick black frames on the left wall—some sepia-toned, others black and white. Tall windows with half-moons on top line the right wall and look out into an enclosed atrium with bonsai, bamboo, stones, and a waterfall pond. From my vantage point, the garden appears to be surrounded by windows, including the rooftop.

We reach a podium where a man and woman wait with warm smiles. "Good evening, sir, miss," the man says. "May I have the name for your reservation?"

"Reed-Alexander," Micah answers.

Why did he put the reservation under both our last names?

There is no time to ponder the answer as the host gathers menus and asks us to follow. He leads us through the restaurant and, as suspected, the entire dining area encompasses the atrium. We are seated at a cloth-covered square table for two. The host lights a single taper candle at the heart of the table, bids us a good evening and steps away.

For a moment, I scan the dining area in slight shock. This place isn't some random place to eat dinner. It is literal fine dining.

Beside the candle is a small vase with a single yellow rose and a sprig of baby's breath. On a spotless white plate in front of me is an intricately folded cloth napkin. More silverware than I use in a day sits on three sides of the plate. A small plate off to the right and two empty wineglasses also fill my place setting.

Not far from where we sit, a wine cellar with a glass front contains several hundred bottles. Chandeliers from the entry—but larger—hang from thick oak beams in the tall ceiling.

"Micah," I whisper across the table. "This place is *too* expensive." I haven't looked at the menu yet, but dinner here feels like hundreds for the two of us.

Micah lays his hand on the table, palm up, and waits for me to take it. Without hesitation, I join our hands. A year has passed and I still feel a jolt when we connect. If anything, the jolt gets stronger with time.

"And as I said before, I wouldn't have brought us if it was too much." He leans in, lifts my hand, and kisses my knuckles in turn. "Let's enjoy the evening. Okay?"

Inhaling a deep breath, I nod. "Yeah. Okay."

Before I pick up the menu, a woman approaches the table in black slacks, a white button-down with a black tie, a black apron tied at the waist that extends below her knees, and a black towel on her forearm.

"Good evening. Welcome to Dusk. Is this your first time dining with us?"

Micah responds with yes and the woman goes into a small story on how the restaurant came to be. Then, she explains the menu. That this is a five-course meal. The menu is a guide for us to choose one of three options for each course. We can choose the same or different. The main course is paired with wine and dessert has beverage options. The dishes are spaced out to give us time to eat and not feel full as each course ends. Once explained, she fills the glasses on the table with water and excuses herself to give us a moment to decide.

I pick up the handheld menu and stare down at the printed card. The options seem simple, but the idea of choosing just one makes me sweat.

"Hey." I peek past the candle to Micah. "It's just dinner." I nod and take a deep breath. "How about we pick different items so we can try more than one."

"Yeah. Sounds good."

When the server returns, we place our full course of options. Micah went with sausage-stuffed roasted cherry tomatoes, spicy tuna tartar, caprese salad, filet mignon, and the chocolate box. I chose the champagne shrimp on endive, caramelized onion and pear tartlets, fig and goat cheese salad, miso-glazed salmon, and berries and cream cake. The server takes our menus and states the hors d'oeuvres will be out shortly before leaving the table.

The moment we are alone, Micah reaches for my hand and I gladly give it.

"This place is more upscale than anywhere else we eat, I know." I lift my brows and pucker my lips, which makes him laugh. "But… today deserves more."

I know what today is, but does he? Not that men should be singled out for forgetting dates, but most men aren't the best at remembering birthdays, anniversaries, or special occasions. At least not the ones from my past.

"It does?" I ask with faux curiosity.

His lips kick up in a half smile. "Don't play the oblivious card with me. You know what today is." My eyes go up and to the right as I shrug. Micah shakes his head and chuckles softly. "As I was saying, today deserves more. Which is why I brought us here." He squeezes my hand. "I never want to take you or our time together for granted. And I plan to celebrate every momentous occasion we share. You're just going to have to deal with it."

I laugh. "Is that an order?"

He tilts his head and half shrugs. "Maybe." He pauses and takes a deep breath. "I love you, Peyton. More than I have loved anyone. And every now and then, I want to spoil you. Take you to nice places and eat fancy meals together. Hope you're okay with that."

More than okay. The longer our relationship is, the more I know the real Micah. See his sensitive and caring side. His protective and defensive side. The man who will yank my hair and choke me one minute and kiss me tenderly as we make love the next.

I love all the facets of Micah Reed. And I love that there are still more to discover.

"Guess I'm okay with it," I tease.

Our time at Dusk passes with small dishes, sampling each other's food, laughter and our hands connected across the table. After we finish dessert and coffee, Micah pays the bill without giving me the slightest notion of cost. Arm in arm, we casually stroll out of the restaurant, wait for the valet to bring the car up, then hop in and drive home.

"Did you have a nice time?" Micah asks as he lifts my hand to his lips and kisses my fingers.

"Yes. The restaurant was wonderful. Thank you." I lean over the console and kiss his cheek.

"You're welcome. And so you know, the night isn't over."

"Good to know." Anniversary sex sounds like a great way to end the evening.

Before long, Micah parks in the driveway and we stroll up the walkway to the house. Not much has changed with the house since I moved in. A few minor details— more flowers in the yard, additional accent pieces inside, picture frames of us and family and friends. I didn't have much furniture of my own and sold it since the house was furnished.

Micah enters the code to unlock the door and steps inside, me on his heels. On the ride home, when Micah said the night wasn't over, I expected him to tear my clothes off when we got home.

But Micah is full of surprises tonight. And the sight before me is beyond expectation.

The entire open floor plan glows. Lit candles rest on every possible surface. As does a plethora of flowers. Every type of yellow flower sits in vases with greenery and baby's breath. I step farther into the room as my eyes dart from one candle and vase to the next.

"When did you? How?" I spin around to find Micah right behind me.

"Shelly."

I turn back to the room and take it all in. Who knew Micah Reed was such a romantic? Over the last year, he has softened around the edges—only on occasion in the bedroom—and I love seeing this side of him.

"This is…"

I whirl around to tell him how romantic this is, but he is no longer eye level. All the air leaves my lungs as I drop my gaze to meet his. Micah, down on one knee, stares up at me as if I hold all of life's secrets.

A hand flies to my mouth as my vision glazes over. "What are you doing?" I choke out.

His soft chuckle floats through the air. "Being romantic. Now, shh." He presses an index finger to his lips for a beat, then reaches for my free hand. My *left* hand.

"Peyton, it's no secret our relationship didn't start in the best light. In all honesty, I was the biggest asshole." We both laugh. "Through all the banter and harsh words, you still called out to me in a way I couldn't ignore. So, I kept up with my persistence. Once I realized who you were and what I'd done all those years ago, I thought there'd be no chance for me." He rubs circles with his thumb over the top of my hand. "But you gave me a chance. You forgave me."

I blink and the first tear rolls down my cheek. Eyes locked on his, I drop my hand from my mouth and nod.

"Slowly, you went from this woman at work I had the hots for to the woman I don't want to live without." I gasp. "Peyton, I don't picture a single day in my future without you. Nor do I want to." He reaches into the pocket of his slacks and takes out a small black box. He flips the lid open and turns the box in his hand. Nestled in the velvet is a platinum band bridal set—the engagement ring with a yellow cathedral round diamond and the wedding band with small white diamonds that hug the engagement stone.

"Oh my god," I whisper in disbelief.

"Peyton Isabel Alexander, I want to spend every day of forever with you. Will you marry me?"

Tears cascade down my cheeks and blur Micah and the room. But my eyes don't leave his. Not for a second. Not as every ounce of love this man holds spills from his heart through his lips.

Micah just asked me to marry him. Never in my life did I imagine this day, this moment.

"Yes," I whisper. "Yes, I'll marry you."

A new smile lights Micah's expression. A love so bright it blinds me. He plucks the engagement ring from the box, lifts my left hand to his lips, kisses my ring finger, then slides the ring into place. Rising from the floor, he wraps his arms around my waist, lifts me off the floor and kisses the hell out of me.

"Thank you," he says when the kiss breaks.

I scrunch my brow. "For what?"

"For you. For saying yes. And for wanting forever with me."

I plant a chaste kiss on his lips. "I love you, Micah Reed."

"And I love you. Future Mrs. Peyton Reed."

He kisses me slow and soft as he walks us to the bedroom. And then, Micah shows me every way he loves me. Now and forever.

Bonus
Content

BONUS CONTENT

MICAH

WHEN I ASKED Peyton to marry me, I had no clue what I was getting myself into.

Leading up to the proposal, I pictured her in a beautiful white gown. Half her hair pinned up with wavy champagne locks trailing down her back. I imagined bright bouquets, hundreds of people in pews with tears in their eyes, cameras flashing, and frankincense in the air.

What I didn't expect was this…

To be standing in the middle of Roar on a Sunday. The club magically overhauled since the door locked less than twenty-four hours ago. The decor is simple yet perfect. Ani and Sean hired an event company to come in and glam up the place for Peyton's and my big day.

Originally, the idea of saying I do to Peyton in the middle of Roar was weird. But Peyton explained it in the simplest of terms.

"This is where we got our second chance. If it weren't for this place, who knows if we would've met again."

I was sold in an instant.

White gauzy fabric hangs from the open ceiling in long torrents, creating strategically placed sheer walls. Countless strands of white fairy lights dangle from metal beams in the ceiling—the only light in the entire space—and float above the small gathering. Twenty collapsible white chairs decorated with the same gauzy fabric sit feet from where I stand. A large copper arch at my back with green vines and the occasional lavender, yellow and white rose tucked between the foliage.

The day after the proposal, I asked Peyton what type of wedding she envisioned for us. How long she wanted to wait for the big day. If she wanted to save for a while and go all out. I expected her to buy one of those wedding organizer books or hire a planner. To purchase bridal magazines and clip pictures of her ideal dress, the perfect bouquet, the dream location, and the ultimate honeymoon.

Did she do a single one of them? Nope.

"I want something simple. We could just elope."

Her words were a shock to the system. Threw me off guard. Peyton never presented herself as someone who wants elaborate or upscale. Not that she doesn't like the finer things. She has just found a way to love the smaller, simpler things in life.

But when you sit down to plan your own wedding, people surprise you. Peyton did; just not in the way I expected.

I convinced her to not elope. Told her our families would never let us live it down. She agreed, thank goodness. But she had one condition—that we not wait.

"What's the point in waiting?"

Which brings us to now. Less than two months after I got down on one knee and asked Peyton to be mine forever. October second.

Soft classical music plays from the speakers overhead. The air smells like I just walked into Shelly's florist shop. Clementine comes into view between the gauzy walls. In a dandelion-yellow sundress, she ambles down the aisle with the biggest smile on her face and sprinkles yellow rose petals on the ground. When she reaches the row where Jonas and Autumn sit, she takes the empty chair between them.

She whisper-asks Autumn, "Did I do good?"

Autumn nods and kisses her daughter's hair.

The music shifts into another classical tune; an unfamiliar song with a sweet, whimsical sound. It starts slow and soft, builds into a stronger harmony, and weaves a web around my heart.

Absolutely perfect.

Two breaths pass before I catch movement on the other side of the gauzy walls. And then I see her.

Peyton comes into view. Reese hooked on her elbow as she walks in my direction. With each step she takes, I remind myself to breathe. To unlock my knees. To carve every second of this moment into my memory.

She has never looked so beautiful.

In a sleeveless ivory gown, intricate lace decorates the bust. Tiny yellow jewels sparkle in the material with each step she takes toward me. In the light of day, I bet she would shine brighter than the sun. The chiffon skirt flows to the floor and glides as if she walks on clouds. Her hair is piled high in an artsy bun with occasional tendrils framing her face. A simple bouquet in her hand with lavender, yellow and white roses and artfully arranged greenery.

When she reaches me and unhooks her arm from Reese's, my heart slips into fifth gear.

This is it. Today, Peyton will tell the world she is mine forever. And I will do the same.

PEYTON

I will not cry. I will not cry.

I chant the words in my head over and over, trying to make them true. But the sting behind my eyes has other plans in store.

The minister drones on with the well-practiced cere-mony. I don't hear any of her words, though. Because every sensory response I own is homed in on the man holding my hands.

Micah Reed.

If a fortune-teller would have told me two years ago, I would marry the man formerly known as my high school antagonist, I would have laughed in their face. I would have demanded my money back and never returned.

But in this moment, as I stare into my favorite starry-sky eyes, I believe all things are possible. Especially redemption.

The minister stops talking and I startle in place. *Time to pay attention, Peyton.*

Micah glances down at my hands a beat before meeting my gaze again. "Fluffy words aren't my strong suit, so bear with me." I laugh, and everyone joins in. "Peyton, I loved you before I truly understood what the word meant. Our beginning started in the darkest of days. And I count my lucky stars each day I wake up next to you. Because you make each day brighter than the last. You make me a better man. A better version of myself. All because you love me too." A devious smile tips up the corners of his mouth. "And I can't wait to call you Mrs. Reed every day of forever."

I laugh through my blurry vision as Micah slips the wedding band on my fourth finger, brings it to his lips, and kisses the band.

"Peyton," the minister chimes in. "When you're ready."

I sniffle and blink a few times. I take a deep breath and swallow.

"Micah Reed..." I chuckle under my breath. "You surprise me at every turn. Who knew my high school crush would one day be my husband." Gasps float through the room as I watch Micah's eyes glaze over. Not everyone knows our history, but enough do. So, to say he was my crush probably shocks them. "The day I walked through these doors and saw you for the first time in years, I never pictured us here." I squeeze his hands harder. "But I wouldn't change a single step of our journey. Because each step we took led us to where we are today. Madly in love. And I can't wait for you to call me Mrs. Reed in the presence of others" —I cock a brow— "and other names when we're alone."

Laughter bursts from Micah's chest as a tear rolls down his cheek. When his eyes meet mine again, I slip a simple platinum band on his ring finger. "I love you, Micah Reed. Today, tomorrow, forever."

The minister prattles on with the final words of the ceremony. But the second she says, "Micah, you may kiss your bride," the room vanishes.

Under the starry lights inside the place that brought Micah and me back together, we kiss as if no one else is in the room. Kiss as if this is the first and last time, wrapped in one. And when the kiss breaks, I stare into my favorite constellation.

"I love you, starlight."

"I love you more, hellcat." He kisses the tip of my nose. "Forever."

More By Persephone Autumn

The Click Duet

High school sweethearts torn apart. When fate gives them a second chance, one doesn't trust they won't be hurt again. Through the Lens (Click Duet #1) and Time Exposure (Click Duet #2) is an angsty, second chance, friends to lovers romance with all the feels.

The Inked Duet

A man with a broken heart and a woman scared to put herself out there. Love is never easy. Sometimes love rips you apart. Fine Line (Inked Duet #1) and Love Buzz (Inked Duet #2) is a second chance at love, single parent romance with a pinch of angst and dash of suspense.

Transcendental

A musician in search of his muse and a woman grieving the loss of her husband. Two weeks at an exclusive retreat and their connection rivals all others. Until she leaves early without notice. But he refuses to give up until he finds her again.

Distorted Devotion

Swept off her feet by love, life takes a dark, unexpected turn. Now the love of her life may be the cause of her death. Check out this gripping, romantic suspense.

Undying Devotion

A long-term couple with a secret life. Their friends envy the bond they share, but remain oblivious to their lifestyle and how deep the bond lies. A turn of events has her wanting to spill every secret.

Beloved Devotion

She asks the love of her life to marry her. When her girlfriend hesitates, then says yes, she is determined to learn why. As the pieces start to fall in place, she discovers she doesn't know her fiancée at all.

Depths Awakened

A small town romance which captivates you from the start. Two broken souls have sworn off love. Vowed to never lose anyone else. But their undeniable attraction brings them together and refuses to let go.

Ink Veins

Persephone Autumn's debut poetry collection, Ink Veins, explores topics of depression, love, and self-discovery with a raw, unfiltered voice.

Broken Metronome

When the music of the heart dies…

Broken Metronome is an angsty poetry collection full of heartache and the possibility of what may have been.

<h1 style="text-align:center;">Thank You</h1>

Thank you so much for reading **A Love So Bright,** book two in the **Insomniac Duet**. If you wouldn't mind taking a moment to leave a review on the retailer site where you made your purchase, Goodreads and/or BookBub, it would mean the world to me.

Reviews help other readers find and enjoy the book as well.

Much love,
	Persephone

Here are some of the songs from the **Insomniac Duet** playlist. You can listen to the entire playlist on Spotify!

overwhelmed | Royal & the Serpent
forget me too | Machine Gun Kelly (f. Halsey)
kiss kiss | machine Gun Kelly
Dancing With A Stranger - Acoustic | Sam Smith,
Normani
Karma | MOD SUN
Wonder - Acoustic | Shawn Mendes
Nightlight | Illenium, Annika Wells
Crazy | TELLE
Her | Majid Jordan
Movement | Hozier

Connect with Persephone

Connect with Persephone

www.persephoneautumn.com

Subscribe to Persephone's Newsletter

www.persephoneautumn.com/newsletter

Join Persephone's Reader Group

Persephone's Playground

Follow Persephone Online

instagram.com/persephoneautumn

facebook.com/persephoneautumnwrites

tiktok.com/@persephoneautumn

goodreads.com/persephoneautumn

bookbub.com/authors/persephone-autumn

amazon.com/author/persephoneautumn

pinterest.com/persephoneautumn

twitter.com/PersephoneAutum

Acknowledgments

So many thank yous, so few pages…

To my family and friends… Thank you for being my favorite cheerleaders. Thank you for pimping my books and telling people I'm an author. And thank you for loving my wild and adventurous brain.

To Ellie McLove and Rosa Sharon… Thank you for your knowledge and brilliance. For all the love notes in the markup area. For your ideas and wise minds when my stories need them most. You ladies make authoring a little less chaotic.

To Kat Savage… Thank you for your cover brilliance and kind heart. Thank you for also being my friend. For listening and talking with me when I needed someone. All the hugs!

To all my author friends… I can't wait to see you all at signing or author conferences and give you a hug. If hugs are cool. Maybe an elbow bump, if that's your thing. I'm just excited to see my peeps again.

To the readers and bloggers who read my words… sending you all virtual hugs. Your reviews and graphics and love give me life. Sharing pieces of yourself with the world is difficult, but your kindness makes it much easier.

And if this is your first Persephone Autumn book… thank you for taking a chance on my words. I hope you loved Micah and Peyton, and the future books to come.

About the Author

Persephone Autumn lives in Florida with her wife, crazy dog, and two lover-boy cats. A proud mom with a cuckoo grandpup. An ethnic food enthusiast who has fun discovering ways to veganize her favorite non-vegan foods. If given the opportunity, she would intentionally get lost in nature.

For years, Persephone did some form of writing; mostly journaling or poetry. After pairing her poetry with images and posting them online, she began the journey of writing her first novel.

She mainly writes romance, but on occasion dips her toes in other works. Look for her poetry publications and a psychological horror under P. Autumn.